Harlequin Romance®
presents a brand-new trilogy from bestselling author

LUCY GORDON

The Counts of Calvani

These proud Italian aristocrats
are about to propose!

The Calvani family is a prosperous, aristocratic
Italian family headed by Count Francesco Calvani.

He has three nephews:
Guido—charming, easygoing and wealthy
in his own right, Guido is based in Venice.
He's heir to the Calvani title, but he doesn't want it....

Marco—aristocratic, sophisticated and very good-
looking, Marco is every woman's dream, managing
the family's banking and investments in Rome.

Leo—proud, rugged and athletic,
Leo is a reluctant tycoon, running the family's
prosperous farms in Tuscany.

The pressure is mounting on all three Calvani brothers
to marry and produce the next heirs
in the Calvani dynasty. Each will find a wife—
but will it be out of love or duty...?

Find out in this emotional,
exciting and dramatic trilogy:

April 2003—*The Venetian Playboy's Bride*
June 2003—*The Italian Millionaire's Marriage*
August 2003—*The Tuscan Tycoon's Wife*

Don't miss it!

Dear Reader,

After Venice, Rome is my favorite Italian city, a place
that once ruled the world, and the Romans still know
it. There is an instinctive pride that makes Roman men,
like Marco Calvani, especially fascinating. They deal
with life on their own terms, and woe betide anyone
who crosses them. Aloof on the surface, they conceal
passion that is irresistible, but only for the right
woman.

Marco, the cool-headed Roman banker, viewed his
cousin Guido's adventures in love with wry amusement,
certain that when his own time came he could keep his
dignity. In *The Italian Millionaire's Marriage* we find him
determined to marry, but not to risk his feelings. He
seeks a marriage of convenience with the granddaughter
of his mother's dearest friend.

Harriet is not what he expected: Half Italian, half
English, she has a passion for antiques. She sees in
Marco a passport to the great art treasures of Rome,
and agrees to an engagement—but only an engagement.
How can this man, who likes to be always in control,
admit to himself that winning her love is growing
more important every day? It is only when he's ready to
cast aside pride and dignity that he finds the courage
to be honest about his feelings. But by then it's almost
too late....

Lucy Gordon

THE ITALIAN MILLIONAIRE'S MARRIAGE

Lucy Gordon

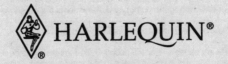

TORONTO • NEW YORK • LONDON
AMSTERDAM • PARIS • SYDNEY • HAMBURG
STOCKHOLM • ATHENS • TOKYO • MILAN • MADRID
PRAGUE • WARSAW • BUDAPEST • AUCKLAND

ISBN 0-373-18097-7

THE ITALIAN MILLIONAIRE'S MARRIAGE

First North American Publication 2003.

Visit us at www.eHarlequin.com

Printed in U.S.A.

PROLOGUE

'I DO not need a husband, do you understand that? I do *not* need a husband. And I certainly don't want one.' These last words were said with a mild shudder that shocked Harriet d'Estino's listener.

'Harriet, calm down,' she begged.

'A *husband?* Good grief! I've lived twenty-seven years without troubling myself with a creature so bothersome and unnecessary—'

'Will you just listen?'

'—and when I find my own sister matchmaking for me— Stars above! You've got a nerve, Olympia.'

'I wasn't matchmaking,' Olympia said placatingly. 'I just thought you might find Marco useful.'

Harriet made a sound that would have been a snort if she hadn't been a lady.

'No man is ever useful,' she said firmly. 'The breed isn't made that way.'

'All right, I won't argue.'

They were half-sisters, one English, one

Italian. Only their rich auburn hair linked them to their common parent, and each other. But in Olympia, the younger, the glorious tresses were teased into a glamorous creation. In Harriet, the same colour hung, straight and austere on either side of an earnest face.

Their clothes too revealed their opposing characters. Olympia was dressed in the height of Italian fashion. Harriet looked as though she'd put on whatever was comfortable and handy. Olympia's figure was slender and seductive. Harriet was certainly slender. It was hard to be sure about anything else.

Olympia looked around her at the exquisite shop in the heart of London's West End. It was filled with fine art and antiques, several of which caught her interest.

'He's splendid,' she exclaimed, noticing a bronze bust of a young man.

'First-century Roman,' Harriet said, glancing up. 'Emperor Caesar Augustus.'

'Really dishy,' Olympia purred, studying the face close up. 'That fine nose, that aristocratic head on the long, muscular neck, and that mouth—all stern discipline masking incredible sensuality. I'll bet he was a tiger with the women.'

'You spend too much time thinking about sex,' Harriet said severely.

'And you don't spend enough time thinking about it. It's disgraceful.'

Harriet shrugged. 'There are more interesting things in life.'

'Nonsense, of course there aren't,' Olympia said with conviction. 'I just wish you were as interested in living men as dead ones.'

'Listen to you!' Harriet riposted. 'You've just been mooning over a man who's been dead for two thousand years. Anyway, dead ones are better. They don't tell lies, get legless or chat up your friends. And you can talk to them without being interrupted.'

'So cynical. Mind you, Marco's pretty cynical, too. Otherwise he'd have married long ago.'

'Aha! He's a grey-beard!'

'Marco Calvani is thirty-five, loaded, and extremely good-looking,' Olympia said emphatically.

'So why aren't you marrying him? You said he asked you first.'

'Only because his mother's an old friend of Pappa's mother, and she's got this sentimental idea of uniting the two families.'

'And he does what she tells him? He's a wimp!'

'Far from it,' Olympia said with a little chuckle. 'Marco is a man who likes his own way all the time. He's doing this for his own reasons.'

'He's a nutter!'

'He's a banker who devotes his life to serious business. He reckons it's time to make a serious marriage and he isn't into courting.'

'He's gay!'

'Not according to my friends. In fact, his reputation is of a ladykiller, with the emphasis on killer. You might say he "loves 'em and leaves 'em" except that he doesn't love 'em. No emotional involvement just a quick fling and goodbye before things get too intense.'

'You make him sound irresistible, you know that?'

'It's only fair to tell you the downs as well as the ups. Marco doesn't go for moonlight and roses, so you can see why he'd be doing this. It would be more of a merger than a marriage, and I thought that since you were serious, too—'

'I'd be happy to take on one of your rejects. Gosh, thanks Olympia.'

'Will you stop being so prickly? I took all this trouble to warn you that he might turn up here next week—'

'And I'm grateful. I've been planning a vacation on the other side of the world. Next week will suit me just fine.'

'Dio mio!' Olympia threw up her hands in sisterly exasperation. 'It's impossible to help some people. You'll end up an old maid.'

Harriet gave a cheeky grin that transformed her face delightfully.

'With any luck,' she said.

CHAPTER ONE

'MY DEAR boy, have you really thought this through?'

Signora Lucia Calvani's face was full of concern as she watched her son lock the suitcase. He gave her a brief smile, warmer for her than for anyone else, but he didn't pause.

'What is there to think through, Mamma? In any case, I'm doing what you required of me.'

'Nonsense! You never do anything except to suit yourself,' she retorted with motherly scepticism.

'True, but it suits me to please you,' Marco replied smoothly. 'You wanted a union between myself and the granddaughter of your old friend, and I consider it suitable.'

'If you mean that you like the idea, kindly say so, and don't address your mother like a board meeting,' Lucia said severely.

'I'm sorry.' He kissed her cheek with a touch of genuine contrition. 'But since I'm doing as you wished I don't understand your concern.'

'When I said I'd like to see you marry Etta's

granddaughter I was thinking of Olympia, as you well know. She's elegant, sophisticated, knows all the right people in Rome, and would have been an admirable wife.'

'I disagree. She's frivolous and immature. Her sister is older and, I gather, has a serious mind.'

'She's been raised English. She may not even speak Italian.'

'Olympia assures me that she does. Her pursuits are intellectual, and she sounds as if she might well suit my requirements.'

'Suit your requirements?' his mother echoed, aghast. 'This is a woman you're discussing, not a block of shares.'

'It's just a way of talking,' Marco said with a shrug. 'Have I forgotten to pack anything?'

He looked around his home which was at its best in the brilliant morning sun that came in through the balcony window. He stepped out for a moment to breathe in the fresh air and enjoy the view along the Via Veneto. From this apartment on the fifth floor of an elegant block he could just make out St Peter's in the distance, and the curve of the River Tiber. In the clear air he caught the sound of bells floating across the city, and he paused a moment to listen and watch the light glinting on the water. He did this every morning, no matter how rushed he might be, and it would have surprised many people who thought of him as a calculating machine and nothing else.

The inside of his home, however, would have reinforced their prejudices. It was costly but spartan, without any softening touch, the home of a man who was enough unto himself. The cool marble of the floors gleamed. The furnishings were largely modern, adorned with one or two valuable old vases and pictures.

It was typical of Marco that he had chosen to live in the centre of Rome, for his heart and mind, his whole presence were Roman. Height, bearing, and the unconsciously arrogant set of his head all spoke of a man descended from a race of emperors.

Nor was it far-fetched to see him as one, for were not international bankers the new emperors? At thirty-five he lorded it over his contemporaries in the financial world. Buying, selling, merging, making deals, these were the breath of life to him, and it was no accident that he spoke of his prospective marriage in a businesslike way that scandalised his mother.

Now he gave her his most charming smile. 'Mamma, I wonder that you dare to reprove me when you yourself proposed the merger.'

'Well, somebody has to arrange proper marriages for this family. When I think of that old fool in Venice, getting engaged to his house-keeper—'

'By "old fool" I take it you mean my Uncle Francesco, Count Calvani, the head of our family,' Marco said wryly.

'Being a count doesn't stop him being an old fool,' Lucia said robustly. 'And being his heir doesn't stop Guido being a young fool, planning to marry an English woman—'

'But Dulcie comes from a titled family, which is very proper,' Marco murmured. He was teasing his mother in his dry way.

'A titled family who've blown every penny on gambling. I've heard the most dreadful stories about Lord Maddox, and I don't suppose his daughter's much better. Bad blood will tell.'

'Don't let either of them hear you criticising their ladies,' Marco warned her. 'They're both in a state of positively imbecile devotion, and will resent it.'

'I've no intention of being rude. But the truth is the truth. Someone has to make a good marriage, and there's no knowing what that bumpkin in Tuscany will do.'

Marco shrugged, recognising his cousin in this description. 'Leo probably won't marry at all. There's no shortage of willing females in the area. I gather he's very much in demand for brief physical relationships on account of—'

'There's no need to be coarse,' Lucia interrupted him firmly. 'If he won't do his duty, all the more reason for you to do yours.'

'Well, I'm off to England to do it. If she suits me, I'll marry her.'

'And if *you* suit *her*. She may not fall at your feet.'

'Then I shall return to you and report failure.'

He didn't sound troubled by the prospect. Marco had found few women who were unimpressed by him. Olympia, of course, had turned him down, but they'd known each other since childhood, and were too much like brother and sister.

'I worry about you,' Lucia said, studying his face and trying to discern what he was really thinking. 'I want to see you with a happy home, instead of always wasting yourself on affairs that don't mean anything. If only you and Alessandra had married, as you should have done. You could have had three children by now.'

'We were unsuited. Let's leave it there.' His voice was gentle but the hint of warning was unmistakable.

'Of course,' Lucia said at once. When Marco's barriers went up even she knew better than to persist.

'It's time I was leaving,' he said. 'Don't

worry, Mamma. I'm simply going to meet Harriet d'Estino and form an impression. If I don't like her I won't mention the idea. She won't know anything about it.'

As he boarded the plane for London Marco reflected that he was behaving unlike himself. He believed in thinking things through, but he was committing an impulsive action.

An *apparently* impulsive action, he corrected the thought. He was an orderly man who lived an orderly life, because success flourished from good order. That meant stability, the correct action performed at the correct time. He'd intended to marry at thirty, and would have done so if Alessandra hadn't changed her mind.

That thought no sooner lived than he killed it. Everything concerning his aborted engagement, including the emotional fool he'd made of himself, was past and done. A wise man learned from experience, and he would never open himself up like that again.

His mother's suggestion of a sensible marriage had been a godsend. To found a family, without involving his heart suited him exactly.

He arrived in London in the late afternoon, taking a suite at the Ritz and spending the rest of the day online, checking various deals that needed his personal attention. The five-hour time difference between America and Europe was too useful to be missed, and it was past midnight before he was through. By that time the Tokyo Stock Exchange was open and he worked until three in the morning. Then he went to bed and slept for precisely five hours, efficiently, as he did everything.

This was how he spent the night before meeting the woman he was planning to make his wife.

He breakfasted on fruit and coffee before setting out to walk the short distance to the Gallery d'Estino. He judged his time precisely, arriving at a quarter to nine, before it was open. This would give him a chance to form an impression of the place before meeting the owner.

What he saw, he approved. The shop was exquisite, and although he could discern little of the merchandise through the protective grilles over the windows, what he could make out seemed well chosen. His mental picture of Harriet d'Estino became clearer: a woman of elegance, *mental* elegance, as well as intellect. He began to warm to her.

The warmth faded a little as nine o'clock passed with no sign of the shop opening. Inefficiency. The unforgivable sin. He turned and collided with someone who yelled, 'Ouch!'

'My apologies,' he murmured to the flustered young woman who was hopping about on the pavement, clutching one foot.

'It's all right,' she said, wincing and nearly losing her balance until Marco took hold of her.

'Thanks. Did you want to go in?'

'Well it is past opening time,' he pointed out.

'Oh, gosh yes, it is, isn't it. Hang on, I've got the key.'

While she scrabbled through a large collection of keys he studied her and found nothing to approve. She wore jeans and a sweater that looked as though they'd been chosen for utility, and a blue woollen hat that covered her hair completely. She might have been young. She might even have been attractive. It was hard to tell since she looked like a worker on a building site. Harriet d'Estino must be desperate for staff to have employed someone so gauche and clumsy.

After what seemed like an age she let him in.

'Just give me a moment,' she said, dumping her packages and starting work on the grilles. 'Then you can have all my attention.'

'Actually I was hoping to see the owner.'

'Won't I do?'

'I'm afraid not.'

The young woman grew suddenly still. Then

she shot him a nervous glance and her whole manner changed.

'Of course, I should have realised. How stupid of me. It's just that I'd hoped for a little more time—that is, *she* hoped for a little more time—I'm afraid Miss d'Estino isn't here just now.'

'Can you tell me when she will be here?' Marco asked patiently.

'Not for ages. But I could give her a message.'

'Could you tell her that Marco Calvani called to see her?'

Her eyes assumed the blankness of someone who was playing 'possum'.

'Who?'

'Marco Calvani. She doesn't know me but—'

'You mean you're not a bailiff?'

'No,' Marco said tersely, with an instinctive glance at his Armani suit. 'I'm not a bailiff.'

'You're sure?'

'I think I'd know if I was a bailiff.'

'Yes,' she said distractedly. 'Of course you would. And you're Italian, aren't you? I can hear your accent now. It's not much of an accent, so I missed it at first.'

'I pride myself on speaking other languages as correctly as possible,' he said, enunciating slowly. 'Would you mind telling me who you are?'

'Me? Oh, I'm Harriet d'Estino.'

'You?' He couldn't keep the unflattering inflection out of his voice.

'Yes. Why not?'

'Because you just told me you weren't here.'

'Did I?' she said vaguely. 'Oh—well—I must have got that wrong.'

Marco stared, wondering if she was mad, bad or merely half-witted. She pulled off the woolly cap, letting her long hair fall about her shoulders, and then he realised that she was speaking the truth, for it was the same rich auburn shade as Olympia's hair. This was the woman he'd been considering as a wife. He took a deep cautious breath.

Harriet was watching him, frowning slightly. 'Have we met before?' she asked.

'I don't believe so.'

'It's just that your face is familiar.'

'We've never met,' he assured her, thinking that he would certainly have remembered.

'I'll make us some coffee.'

Harriet went into the back of the shop and put on the coffee, annoyed with herself for having made a mess of everything after Olympia's warning. But she'd half convinced herself that Marco wouldn't bother coming to see her, and her mind had been so taken up with worries about her creditors that she'd had little time to think of other things.

As an expert in antiquities Harriet had no rival. Her taste was impeccable, her instincts flawless, and many an imposing institution accepted her opinion as final. But somehow she couldn't translate this skill into a commercial profit, and the bills were piling up.

The coffee perked and she brought herself back to reality. She would have given anything not to have betrayed her money worries to this man, but perhaps he hadn't noticed. Then he appeared beside her and she became distracted by the resemblance. Just where had she seen him before?

She'd promised Olympia not to let Marco suspect that she'd been forewarned, so it might be safest to play dumb for a while. It was a melancholy fact, she'd discovered, that if you pretended to be really stupid people always believed you.

'Why did you want to see me, Signor—Calvani, was it?'

'My name means nothing to you?'

'I'm sorry, should it?'

'I'm a friend of your sister Olympia. I thought she might have mentioned me.'

'We're only half-sisters. We grew up far

apart and don't see each other often.' She added casually, 'How is she these days?'

'Still the beautiful social butterfly. I told her I'd look you up while I was in London. If it's agreeable to you we might spend this evening together, perhaps go to a show and have dinner afterwards.'

'That would be nice.'

'What kind of show do you like?'

'I've been trying to get into *Dancing On Line*, but the seats are like gold-dust and tonight's the last performance.'

'I think I might manage it, just the same.'

She was conscience stricken. 'If you're thinking of the black market, the tickets are going for thousands. I shouldn't have said anything.'

'I shan't need to resort to the black market,' he said, smiling.

She regarded him with something approaching awe. 'You can get seats for this show, at a moment's notice?'

'I can't afford to fail now, can I?' he remarked, somewhat wryly. 'Leave it to me. I'll collect you here at seven.'

'Fine. And we can always go to a different show. I really don't mind.'

'We shall go to this show and no other,' he said firmly. 'Until tonight.'

'Until tonight,' she said, a trifle dazed.

He turned to the door, but stopped as though something had just occurred to him.

'By the way, I believe in mixing business with pleasure. Perhaps you would look at this and value it for me.'

From his bag he drew a package which he unwrapped before her eager eyes, revealing a fabulously beautiful ornate necklace in sold gold. She took it gently and carried it to a desk, switching on a brilliant light.

'I have a friend in Rome who specialises in these things,' Marco said smoothly. 'He thinks this is one of the best Greek pieces he's ever seen.'

'Greek?' she said, not raising her eyes. 'Oh, no, Etruscan.'

She'd passed the first test, but he concealed his pleasure and pressed her further.

'Are you sure? My friend is a real expert.'

'Well it can be difficult to tell them apart,' she conceded. 'Etruscan goldsmiths of the archaic and classical periods...'

She was away and there was no stopping her, he recognised. Words poured out. 'Their jewellery of the third to first centuries BC often closely resembles Greek works but—Celtic influence—'

He listened with growing satisfaction. She might be a little strange but here was the educated lady he'd hoped for. This fabulous piece had been in his family's possession for two centuries. It was pure Etruscan. And she'd spotted it.

Then she blew his satisfaction out of the water by saying regretfully, 'If only it were real.'

He stared. 'Of course it's real.'

'No, I'm afraid not. It's a very good copy, one of the best I've ever seen. I can understand why it fooled your friend—'

'But not you,' he said, feeling illogically annoyed at her slander of his non-existent 'friend'.

'I've always taken a special interest in artefacts from Etruria,' she said, naming the province that had later become Rome and its surrounding countryside. 'I visited a dig there a couple of years back and it was the most fascinating—'

'And this qualifies you to pronounce on this piece?' Marco interrupted, his annoyance overcoming his good manners.

'Look, I know what I'm talking about, and frankly this "expert" of yours doesn't, since he can't tell Greek from Etruscan.'

'But according to you it's a fake which means it can't be either,' he pointed out.

'It's a copy, and whoever did it was copying an Etruscan piece, not a Greek one,' she said firmly.

The transformation in her was astonishing, he thought. Gone was the awkward young woman who'd collided with him at the door. In her place was an authority, steely, assured, implacable in her own opinion. He would have found it admirable if she wasn't trying to wipe a million dollars off his fortune.

'Are you saying that this is worthless?' he demanded.

'Oh, not entirely worthless. The gold must be worth something.'

She spoke in the manner of an adult placating a disappointed child, and he ground his teeth.

'Would you like to explain your opinion?' he said frostily.

'All my instincts tell me that this isn't the real thing.'

'You mean feminine intuition?'

'Certainly not,' she said crisply. 'There's no such thing. Funny, I'd have expected a man to know that. My instincts are based on knowledge and experience.'

'Which sounds like another name for female intuition to me. Why not be honest and admit it?'

Her eyes flashed, magnificently. 'Signor Whatever-Your-Name-Is—if you just came in here to be offensive you're wasting your time. The weight of this necklace is wrong. A genuine

Etruscan necklace would have weighed just a little more. Did you know that scientific tests have proved that Etruscan gold was always the same precise weight, and—?'

She was away again, facts and figures tumbling out of her mouth at speed, totally assured and in command of her subject. Except that she was completely wrong, he thought grimly. If this was the level of her expertise it was no wonder her business was failing.

'Fine, fine,' he said trying to placate her. 'I'm sure you're right.'

'Please don't patronise me!'

He was about to respond in kind when he checked himself, wondering where his wits were wandering. When he'd considered this encounter his plans hadn't included letting her needle him to the point of losing his temper. Coolness was everything. That was how victories were won, deals were made, life was organised to advantage. And she'd blown it away in five minutes.

'Forgive me,' he said with an effort. 'I didn't mean to be impolite.'

'Well, I suppose it's understandable, considering how much poorer I've just left you.'

'I don't accept that you have left me poorer, since I don't accept your valuation.'

'I can understand that you wouldn't,' she said

in a kindly voice that took him to the limit of exasperation. She handed him back the necklace. 'When you return to Rome why don't you ask your friend to take another look at this? Only don't believe a word he says because he doesn't know the difference between Greek and Etruscan.'

'I'll collect you here at seven o'clock,' Marco said, from behind a tight smile.

CHAPTER TWO

SEVEN o'clock found Harriet peering out of her shop window into a storm. She'd been home, dressed for an evening out and returned in a hurry, not wishing to keep him waiting.

But it seemed he had no such qualms about her. Five past seven came and went, then ten, and there was no sign of him. At seven-fifteen she muttered something unladylike and prepared to leave in a huff.

She'd just locked the door and was staring crossly at the downpour when a cab came to a sharp halt at the kerb, a door opened and a hand reached out from the gloom within. She took it, and was seized in a powerful grip, then drawn swiftly inside.

'My apologies for being late,' Marco said. 'I took a cab because of the rain and found myself trapped. Luckily the show doesn't start until eight, so even at this crawl we should make it in time.'

'You don't mean to say that you managed it?' Harriet asked incredulously.

'Certainly I managed it. Why should you doubt me?'

'Who did you blackmail?'

Marco grinned. 'It was a little more subtle than that. Not much, but a little.'

'I'm impressed.'

She grew even more impressed when she discovered that he'd secured the best box in the house. No doubt about it. This was a man with good contacts.

Marco offered her the chair nearer the stage so that he was a little to the rear and could glance at her as well as the show. She wasn't beautiful, he decided. Her slenderness went, perhaps, a little too far: not thin he assured himself hastily, but as lean as a model. Elegant. Or, at least, she would be if she worked on her appearance, which she clearly didn't.

Her chiffon evening gown was all right, no more. It descended almost to her shapely ankles, and clung slightly, revealing the grace of her movements. The deep red was a magnificent shade, but it was exactly wrong with her auburn hair, which she wore loose and flowing. She should have put it up, he thought, revealing her face and emphasising her long neck. Was there nobody to tell her these things?

Her few pieces of jewellery were poorly chosen and didn't really go well together. She should wear gold, he decided. Not delicate pieces, but powerful, to go with her aura of quiet strength. He would enjoy draping her with gold.

The thought reminded him of the necklace, but he was in a good humour now, and bore her no ill will. If anything, their spat had been useful in breaking the ice.

Dancing On Line was a very modern musical, a satire about the internet, dry, witty, with good tunes and sharp dancers. They both enjoyed it, and left the theatre in a charity with one another. The rain had stopped, and the cab he'd ordered was waiting.

'I know a small restaurant where they do the best food in London,' he said.

He took her to a place that she, a Londoner, had never heard of. Slightly to her surprise it was French, not Italian, but then she realised that surprise was the name of the game. If he really was planning an outrageous suggestion then it made sense for him to confuse her a little first.

'Perhaps I should have asked if you like French food,' he said when they had seated themselves at a quiet corner table.

'I like it almost as much as Italian,' she said, speaking in French. It might be showing off but she felt that flying all her flags would be a good idea.

'Of course you're a cosmopolitan,' he said. 'In your line of work you'd have to be. Spanish?'

'Uh-uh! Plus Greek and Latin.'

'Modern Greek or classical?'

'Both of course,' she said, contriving to sound faintly shocked.

'Of course.' He smiled faintly and inclined his head in respect.

The food really was the best. Harriet notched up a mark to him. He was an excellent host, consulting her wishes while making suggestions that didn't pressure her. She let him pick the wine, and his choice exactly suited her.

The light was dim in their corner, with two small wall lamps and two candles in glass bowls on the table, making shadows dance and flicker. Even so she managed to study his face and had to give him ten out of ten for looks. His dinner jacket was impeccable, and his white, embroidered evening shirt made a background for his lightly tanned skin. He was a handsome man. She conceded that. His lips, perhaps, were slightly on the thin side, but in a way that emphasised his infrequent smiles, giving them a quirky irony that pleased her.

His eyes drew her attention, being very dark

brown, almost black. She would have called them beautiful if the rest of his face hadn't been so unmistakably masculine. They were deep set and slightly shadowed by a high forehead and heavy eyebrows. That gave his face a hint of mystery, because she couldn't always see whether his eyes had the same expression as his mouth. And she suspected that they often didn't.

So far, so intriguing. It was lucky Olympia had warned her what was afoot, or she might have been completely taken in; might actually have found him seriously attractive. As it was, she held the advantage. She decided to disconcert him a little, just for fun.

'What brings you to London?' she asked innocently. 'Business?'

If the question threw him he gave no sign of it. 'A little. And I must pay my respects to Lady Dulcie Maddox, who became engaged to my cousin Guido a few weeks ago.'

Harriet savoured the name. 'Lord Maddox's daughter?'

'Yes, do you know her?'

'She's been in the shop a couple of times.'

'Buying or selling?'

'Selling.' Harriet fell silent, sensing a minefield.

'Probably pieces from the Maddox ancestral

home, to pay her father's debts,' Marco supplied. 'I gather he's a notorious gambler.'

'Yes,' she said, relaxing. 'I didn't want to tell tales if you didn't know.'

'It's common knowledge. Dulcie has to earn her living, and she was working as a private enquiry agent when she came to Venice and met Guido. What did you think of her?'

'Beautiful,' Harriet said enviously. 'All that long fair hair—if she still has it?'

'She had when I said goodbye to her a few weeks back. As you say, she's beautiful, and she'll keep Guido in order.'

She laughed. 'Does he need keeping in order?'

'Definitely. A firecracker, with no sense of responsibility. That's my Uncle Francesco talking, by the way. Count Calvani. He's been desperate for Guido to marry and produce an heir to the title.'

'Hasn't he done that himself?'

'No, the title will go to one of his nephews. It should have been Leo, Guido's older half-brother. Their father married twice. His first wife, Leo's mother, was supposedly a widow, but her first husband turned up alive, making the marriage invalid and Leo illegitimate, and unable to inherit the title.'

'That's dreadful!'

'Leo doesn't think so. He doesn't want to be a count. The trouble is, neither does Guido, but that's going to be his fate. So uncle tried to find him a suitable wife, and was giving up in despair when Guido fell for Dulcie.

'My uncle is also, finally, going to get married. Apparently he's been in love with his housekeeper for years and has finally persuaded her to marry him. He's in his seventies, she's in her sixties, and they're like a pair of turtle-doves.'

'That's charming!' Harriet exclaimed.

'Yes, it is, although not everyone thinks so. My mother is scandalised that he's marrying "a servant" as she calls her.'

'Does anyone care about that kind of thing these days?'

'Some people,' Marco said carefully. 'My mother's heart is kind but her views about what is "proper" come from another age.'

'What about you?'

'I don't always embrace modern ways,' he said. 'I make my decisions after a lot of careful thought.'

'A banker would have to, of course.'

'Not always. Among my banking colleagues I have the reputation of sometimes getting carried away.'

'You?' she asked with an involuntary emphasis.

'I have been known to thrown caution to the winds,' he said gravely.

'Profitably, of course.'

'Of course.'

She studied his face, trying to see if he was joking or not, unable to decide. He guessed what she was doing and regarded her wryly, eyebrows raised as if to ask whether she'd worked it out yet. The moment stretched on and he grew uncomfortably aware of something transfixed in her manner.

'Would you like some more wine?' he asked, to bring her back to earth.

'I'm sorry, what was that?'

'Wine.'

'Oh, no—no, thank you. You know your face really is familiar. I wish I could remember—'

'Perhaps I remind you of a boyfriend,' he suggested delicately. 'Past or present?'

'Oh, no, I haven't had a boyfriend for ages,' she murmured, still regarding him.

What was the matter with her he wondered? Sophisticated one minute, gauche the next. Still, it told him what he needed to know.

As they were eating he asked, 'How do you and Olympia come to have different nationalities?'

'We don't,' Harriet said quickly. 'We're both Italian.'

'Well, yes, in a sense—'

'In every sense,' she interrupted with a touch of defiance. 'I was born in Italy, my father is Italian and my name is Italian.'

'I'm sorry,' Marco said, seeing the glint of anger in her large eyes and thinking how well it suited her. 'I didn't mean to offend you.'

'Hasn't Olympia told you the story?'

'Only vaguely. I know your father married twice, but naturally Olympia knows very little about his first wife.'

'My mother loved him terribly and he just dumped her. I remember when I was five years old, finding her crying her eyes out. She told me he was throwing us out of the house.'

'Your mother told you that?' he echoed, genuinely shocked. 'A child?'

'She was distraught. I simply didn't believe it. I adored my father and he acted as though he adored me. He used to call my name first when he came home. I thought it would always be like that.'

'Go on,' he said gently, when she paused.

'Well, his girlfriend was pregnant and he wanted a quick divorce so that he could marry her before the child was born. We were out. Mum said he even forced her to go back to

England by threatening to be mean about money if she didn't.'

Marco thought of Guiseppe d'Estino, a fleshy, self-indulgent man of great superficial charm but cold eyes, as he now realised. He could well believe this story.

'It must have been a sad life for you after that,' he said sympathetically.

'I kept thinking he'd invite me for a visit, but he never did. I couldn't understand what I'd done to turn him against me. My mother never recovered. She grieved every day of her life. She only lived another twelve years, then she had heart trouble and just faded away. I thought he'd send for me then, but he didn't. I was about to go to college and he said he didn't want to interrupt my education.'

Marco murmured something that might have been a swear word.

'Yes,' Harriet said wryly. 'I suppose I was beginning to get the picture then, very belatedly. I was rather stupid about it really.'

'The one thing nobody could ever call you is stupid,' Marco said, regarding her with new interest. 'I know that much about you.'

'Oh, *things*,' she said dismissively. 'Anyone can learn about things. I'm stupid about people. I don't really know much about them.'

'Or maybe you know too much about the

wrong sort of people,' he said, thinking of the father who'd selfishly cast her off, and the mother who'd made the child bear the burden of her grief. 'Did your father totally reject you?'

'No, he kept up a reasonable pretence when he couldn't help it. I studied in Rome for a year. I chose that on purpose because I knew he'd have to take some notice of me. I even thought he might invite me to stay.'

'But he didn't?'

'I was asked to dinner several times. His second wife sat and glared at me the whole time, but Olympia was always nice. We got quite friendly. After that my father sent me a cheque from time to time.'

'Did he help you buy the shop?'

'No, that was money I inherited from my mother's father. I was able to buy the lease and some stock.'

'Your father could have afforded to help you. He ought to have stood up to that woman.'

'You mean his wife? Do you know her?'

'And detest her. As do most people. Of course she was determined to keep you out. My poor girl. You never stood a chance.'

'I guess I know that now. But at the time I thought I could win him over by doing well, learning languages, passing exams, being as Italian as possible.'

Marco was growing interested in her strange upbringing. He suspected it had moulded her into an unusual person.

'Did you really think I was a bailiff?' he asked curiously.

'For a moment.' She gave a gruff little laugh. 'You'd think I'd know how to recognise them by now. I keep thinking things will get better—well, they do. But then they get bad again.'

'But why? That shop should be a gold-mine. Your stock is first-rate. It's true, you made a mistake about the necklace, but—'

'I did *not* make—never mind. Sometimes I get on top of the figures, but then I see this really beautiful piece that I just have to have, and bang go all my calculations.'

'Why not just sell up?'

'Sell my shop? Never. It's my life.'

He ran up a flag. 'There's more to life than antiques.'

She shot it down. 'No, there isn't.'

'You seem very sure of that.'

'It's not just antiques, it's—it's the other worlds they open up. Vast horizons were you can see for thousands of years—'

She was away again. Recognising that it would be impossible to halt the flow until she was ready Marco settled for listening with the top part of his brain, while the rest considered her.

He'd grown more agreeably impressed as the evening wore on. She was an intriguing companion, intelligent, educated, even witty. It was a shame that she wasn't beautiful—at least, he thought she probably wasn't. It was hard to be sure when her hair shielded so much of her face. But her green eyes flashed fire when she spoke of the 'other worlds' that she loved, and in them was a kind of beauty.

Her lapses into gaucheness were hardly her fault. She'd been denied the chance to grow up in sophisticated society. A few trips to the discreetly luxurious shops on the Via dei Condotti would greatly improve her. He felt he had the basis for a deal that would be beneficial on both sides.

Harriet was bringing her passionate arguments to a conclusion. 'You don't think I'm crazy, do you?' she asked anxiously.

'You care passionately about your subject,' he said. 'That isn't being crazy. It's being lucky. So saving your shop means more to you than anything in the world, and perhaps I can help. How much would it take to extricate you from your difficulties?'

She named a large sum with the air of someone plunging into the deep end.

'It's a lot,' Marco said wryly, 'but not too much. I think we're in a position to help each other. I can make you an interest-free loan that will solve your problems.'

'But why should you?'

'Because I want something in return.'

'Naturally. But what?'

He hesitated. 'You may find this suggestion a little unusual, but I've considered it carefully, and I assure you it makes sense for both of us. I want you to come to Rome with me, and be my mother's guest for a while.'

'Are you sure she'll want that?'

'She'll be delighted. Your paternal grandmother was her dearest friend, and her hope is that our families can become united. In short, she's trying to arrange my marriage.'

'Who with?' Harriet asked, not wanting to seem to understand too much too soon.

'With you.'

She'd known that this moment was coming, but without warning she was embarrassed. Watching him sitting there in the corner, the candlelight on his face, he was suddenly too much; too forceful, too attractive, too like an irresistible gale storming through her life, flattening all before it. Too *much*.

'Hey, hold on,' she said, playing for time. 'Things aren't done like that these days.'

'In some societies marriages are still arranged—or at least, half arranged. Suitable people are introduced and the benefits of an alliance considered. My parents' marriage was created like this, and it was very happy. They were compatible, but not blinded by emotions too intense to last.'

'And you're asking me—?'

'To think about it. The final decision can be taken later, when we know each other better. In the meantime I'll sort out your financial problems. Should we make a match I'll wipe the loan out. If not we'll part friends, and you can repay me on easy terms.'

'Whoa there! You're going too fast. I can't take this in.' It was true. She'd thought herself well prepared, but everything was so different to her imaginings that it was taking her breath away.

'You can't lose. At the worst you get an interest-free loan that will save your shop.'

'But what's in it for you?' she demanded bluntly. 'You can't get married just to please your mother.'

It seemed to her that he hesitated a fraction, then answered with a little constraint. 'I can *if that is what I wish*. It's time for me to have a settled life, with a family, and it suits me to arrange it in this way.'

'It will give us both time to think,' he went on. 'You return with me, try out life in my country—*your* country, and consider whether you'd enjoy it permanently. If you and my mother get on well, we'll discuss marriage.'

'What about you and me getting on well?'

'I hope we may, since we could hardly have a successful marriage otherwise. I'm sure you'll be an excellent mother to our children, and after that you won't find me unreasonable.'

'Unreasonable about what?' she asked, beginning to get glassy eyed.

'Come, we're not adolescents. We needn't interfere with each other's freedom as long as we're discreet.'

She tried to study his face, but it was hard because his eyes were in shadow.

'Don't you mind doing it this way?' she asked at last. 'Don't you have any feelings about it?'

'There's no need for us to discuss feelings,' he said, suddenly distant.

'But you've got everything planned like a business deal.'

'Sometimes that can achieve optimum results.'

The cool precision of his tone sent a frisson of alarm through her. For the first time she understood the extent to which he'd banished human warmth from this plan, and it gave her a sense of unreality. Only a man who'd built fences around himself could act like this. She wondered how high the fences were, and why he needed them.

And what about your own fences? murmured an inner voice. You know they're there. Brains are safe. Your head can't hurt you like your heart can. Maybe you're two of a kind, and he sensed it?

She quickly rejected the idea, but it lingered, troubling her, refusing to be totally dismissed.

Playing for time, she said, 'If we married you'd expect me to come to live with you, right?'

He looked slightly startled. 'That is the usual arrangement.'

'But if I move to Rome I'll lose the shop that I'm trying to save.'

'You can leave your establishment here and have it run by a manager, or move it to Rome. You might even find it helpful to be there. I'm sure there's a great deal you haven't explored yet.'

He'd touched a nerve. Not meeting his eyes Harriet said, 'I suppose you know everybody.'

'Not quite everybody. But I know a lot of people who could be useful to you.'

He would know Baron Orazio Manelli, she

thought. He'd probably been in the Palazzo Manelli, with its vast store of hidden treasures. Harriet had been writing to the Baron for two years now, seeking permission to study that Aladdin's cave. And for two years he had barred her entry. But as Marco's fiancée…

She bid the tempter be silent, but he whispered to her of bronze and gold, of ancient jewellery and historic sculptures.

'A visit,' she said. 'With neither of us committed.'

'That's understood.'

'We might simply decide it wouldn't work.'

'And part friends. But in the meantime my mother would have the pleasure of your company.'

Torn between conscience and temptation she stared at his face as though hoping to find the answer there. And then, against all odds, she did.

'That's it!' she breathed. 'Now I know where I've seen your face.'

'I'm glad,' he said, amused. 'Who do I remind you of?'

'Emperor Caesar Augustus.'

'I beg your pardon!'

'I've got him in the shop—his bust in bronze. It's your face.'

'Nonsense. That's pure fancy.'

'No it's not. Come on, I'll show you.'

'What?'

'Let's go and see. We've finished eating, haven't we?'

He'd planned a leisurely liqueur or two, but he could tell it would be simpler to yield. 'Yes, we've finished,' he agreed.

He was a man who led while others followed, but he found himself swept along by her urgent enthusiasm until they were back in her shop, and she'd turned the lights on the bust.

'Now is that you or isn't it?' she demanded triumphantly.

'No,' he said, astounded. 'There's no resemblance at all. You brought me all the way back here to look at that?'

'I'm not imagining it. That's you. Look again. Look.'

He didn't look. Instead he gave a soft laugh, as though something had mysteriously delighted him, and came to stand in front of her, putting one hand on her shoulder. With the other he lifted her chin so that he could look into her eyes. She could feel his warm breath against her skin, whispering across her mouth so that a tiny shiver went through her. But although their faces were so close, he didn't lower his head, only gave her a small, intriguing smile.

'A sensible man would run for his life at this point,' he said wryly.

'And you're a very sensible man, aren't you?'

He brushed back a stray wisp of hair. 'Maybe I'm not as sensible as I thought I was. I know you're not a sensible woman. You're completely crazy.'

'I suppose I am. A woman who wasn't crazy wouldn't even consider your idea.'

'True. Then I must be grateful.' He looked down into her face, still smiling, still meeting her eyes.

Then something happened that shocked her. His smile faded. He released her and stepped back. 'Can you be ready to leave in two days?' he asked with cool courtesy.

She was too stunned to speak. One moment her body had been vibrating from the intimacy of his closeness, his hands, his breath. The next, it was all over, and by his choice, that was clear. He'd deliberately slammed the door shut on whatever might have happened between them next.

She pulled herself together and replied in a voice that matched his own. 'Speaking as a businesswoman, will I have the money by then?'

'You will have it by midday tomorrow.'

'But you haven't seen my books,' she said, suddenly conscience stricken.

'Do I need to? I'm sure they're terrible.'

'Suppose you can't afford me?'

'I assure you that I can.'

She gave a sharp little laugh, half-tension, half-anger. 'Then perhaps I should marry you for your money.'

'I thought that was what we'd been discussing.'

She surveyed him defiantly, arms folded. 'I can't put one over on you, can I?'

'I try to ensure that nobody can. It's the best way to achieve—'

'*Optimum results.*' She said the words with him, and he gave her a nod of respect.

'Let me take you home,' he said.

'No thank you.' Anger had faded as she realised that the threat to the thing she loved most in the world had gone. With a sudden beatific smile that startled him she said, 'I want to be alone here for a while. Now that it's safe.'

'I'll wait for you outside,' he said firmly. 'It's midnight, and I won't leave you alone with these valuables, a target for robbers and worse. Your untimely death wouldn't suit me at all.'

'No, you'd have to rethink the whole plan,' she agreed affably.

He took her hand. 'It's a pleasure to do business with someone who understands what matters. I'll be outside.'

He held her hand for a moment, then raised it and brushed his lips against the back before walking out.

Left alone, Harriet looked down at her hand, where she could still feel the light imprint of his mouth. She was shaken and her heart was beating either with pleasure or apprehension, she wasn't sure. She could only do this if she felt in control, and he'd threatened that control. Furiously she rubbed the back of her hand until the feeling had gone.

Then she looked around her and her eyes shone. Safe. At least for a while.

The tempter was there again, whispering that the 'engagement' could last just long enough for her to investigate the Palazzo Manelli, and no longer. And why not? The plan would be heartless if Marco's feelings had been involved, but he'd been at pains to emphasise that they weren't. He'd looked her over as a piece of merchandise that he could make use of, so why shouldn't she do the same with him?

She knew another brief flare of resentment at the way he'd drawn close to her then backed off. A man who was so much in control of himself wouldn't be easy to deal with. If she let

him, he would call all the shots. But she
wouldn't let him.

His face came into her mind and her eyes fell
on the bronze face of Augustus, the two so exactly alike—whatever Marco thought. She remembered Olympia's words, 'Really dishy.
That fine nose, and that mouth—all stern discipline masking incredible sensuality.'

It was true, Harriet realised. The wonder was
that she alone had seen it in the living man.

CHAPTER THREE

DURING the next couple of days the whirl of arrangements was so intense that she had no time to think. Marco inspected the shop's books, groaned at her business practices—'pure Alice in Wonderland'—but advanced a money order that cleared her debts. It also left her something over to pay extra to Mrs Gilchrist, her excellent manager, who was to take sole charge.

There was one tense moment when Harriet brought a customer to the verge of buying a very expensive piece, only to start talking it down until he lost interest and left the shop empty handed.

'There was nothing the matter with it,' declared Marco, who had watched, aghast.

'I didn't like him.'

'What?'

'He wouldn't have given it a good home,' she tried to explain. 'You don't understand do you?'

'Not a word!' he said grimly.

'These aren't just things I buy and sell. I love

them. Would you sell a puppy to a man you
thought wouldn't be kind to it?'

'Harriet, puppies are alive. These things are
not.'

'Yes they are, in their own way. I won't sell
something to a person I don't trust.'

'You madwoman. You've got windmills in
your head. Let's leave this place while I can still
stand it.'

They left next day on the midday flight to
Rome. Signora Lucia Calvani was waiting for
them, and the moment she saw Harriet her face
lit up.

'Etta,' she cried, advancing with her arms
open. 'My dear, dear Etta.'

Enveloped in a scented embrace Harriet felt
a lump come to her throat at this unexpected
welcome.

'You know why I call you Etta, don't you?'
Lucia asked, taking her shoulders and standing
back a little.

'My father used to call me that, when I was
a little girl,' Harriet said eagerly. 'He said it was
because of his mother—'

'Yes, her name was Enrichetta, but people
called her Etta. I did, when we were girls together. Oh, you're so like her.' She hugged
Harriet again.

Her greeting to her son was restrained but her

eyes left no doubt that he was the centre of her life. Then she immediately turned her attention back to her guest, drawing Harriet's arm through her own and leading her towards the chauffeur-driven Rolls-Royce.

Their route lay out in the countryside, giving Rome a wide sweep until they were south of the city and hit the Via Appia Antica, the ancient road alongside which stood the ruins of tombs of aristocratic Roman families, going back a thousand years. Here too were the mansions of their modern counterparts. They stood well back from the road, hidden behind high walls and elaborate metal gates, housing families who quietly ran the world. A Calvani could live nowhere else.

Signora Calvani was a beautiful, exquisite woman with white hair, dressed in the height of Roman fashion. Harriet guessed her to be about seventy, but with her tall, slender figure and elastic walk she could have been younger. Her voice and gestures were those of someone who'd always been surrounded by money.

'I was so delighted when Marco said you were to pay us a visit,' she said as the car glided through the countryside. 'The house seems very empty sometimes.'

They had passed the wrought-iron gates of the villa and were gliding between trees until the Villa Calvani came into view suddenly. It was a huge white house with flower-hung balconies and broad steps rising to the double front door, and Harriet could understand how it must seem empty to someone who lived there alone.

An unseen servant opened the front door and Lucia led her graciously into the hall, and from there into a large salon. A maid appeared to take Harriet's coat. Another maid wheeled in a tea trolley.

'English tea,' Lucia declared. 'Especially for you.'

As well as tea there were sweet biscuits and savouries, sandwiches, cakes. Whatever her taste it was catered for. For a while they exchanged standard pleasantries, but behind the questions Harriet sensed that Lucia's real attention was elsewhere. She was studying her guest, and was evidently delighted with what she found. It was a welcome such as Harriet had never received in her life. Marco was looking pleased as the extent of his mother's warmth became clear.

'Now I'll show you your room,' Lucia said, rising.

Her room was even more overwhelming, with floor-length windows that looked out onto the magnificent Roman countryside. Harriet could see a river and pine trees stretching into the distance, all glowing in the afternoon sun.

The bed was big enough for three, an elaborate confection of carved walnut with a tapestry cover. The floor was polished wood, and the furniture was old-fashioned with the walnut theme repeated. The ornaments were traditional pieces, carved heads, pictures, some of them valuable Harriet automatically noted with a professional eye.

But she didn't want to think about work just now. She was basking in the feeling of being wanted, so unfamiliar to her.

'Do you think you'll be comfortable here?' Lucia asked kindly. 'Would you like anything changed?'

'It's all beautiful,' Harriet said huskily. 'I've never—' To her dismay a sudden rush of tears choked her and she had to turn away.

'But whatever is the matter?' Lucia asked in alarm. 'Marco, have you been unkind to her?'

'Certainly not,' he said at once.

'Nobody's been unkind,' Harriet said huskily. 'On the contrary, you've all—I've never—'

'It's time I was getting back to my work,' Marco said, looking uncomfortable. 'I've neglected it too long—'

'What do you mean "too long"?' his mother demanded, scandalised.

'I beg your pardon, and Harriet's. I didn't mean to be impolite. But I really must return to my office, and then to my own apartment for a few days.'

'You aren't coming to supper tonight?' Lucia demanded. 'It's Etta's first evening with us.'

'Regretfully I must decline that pleasure. I'll call soon and let you know when to expect me.'

He kissed his mother and, after a moment's hesitation, kissed Harriet's cheek. Then he departed hastily.

'Such manners!' Lucia exclaimed.

'Well, I've already gathered that he's a workaholic,' Harriet admitted. 'And I suppose he must have lost a lot of time.'

'You and I will spend the next few days getting to know each other.' Lucia seized Harriet's hands. 'I am *so* happy.'

Harriet's feeling of having landed unexpectedly in heaven showed no sign of abating. Lucia had ordered various English dishes to please her and proudly put them on display when they dined together that evening.

'For of course I realise that you are *partly* English,' she explained, with the air of someone making a generous concession. 'But Italian in your heart, *si*?'

'*Si*,' Harriet agreed, wondering just how

much Marco had told her. Lucia's eyes were full of understanding.

From then on she switched to the Italian language, and in no time they were the best of friends.

'Why not call your father to let him know that you're here?' Lucia asked.

Harriet felt a strange reluctance, as though there was something to be feared, but she went to the telephone and called her father's number. She was answered by an unfamiliar voice, a man, who explained that Signor d'Estino and his family were away for several days. Nor would he divulge their destination, even when Harriet explained that she was his daughter. It was clear that he had never heard of her. She left a message, asking her father to call, and hung up, refusing to let herself feel pain.

The next morning Harriet arose refreshed, to find that Lucia had planned their day. 'We'll have lunch in town,' she said, 'and just look around.'

It was a joy to Harriet to renew her acquaintance with Rome, the great city that lived in her dreams. Once it had been the centre of the known world. Now it was a place of traffic jams and tourists, yet still dominated by glorious ancient monuments. After lunch they strolled along the luxurious Via Veneto, and Lucia pointed out Marco's apartment, high up on the fifth floor. Harriet looked up at the windows, but they were closed and shuttered. Like the man himself, she thought.

She spent the next day alone as Lucia was on several charity committees and had meetings to attend. Now she could reclaim Rome in her own way. Happily she wandered its cobbled streets, exploring narrow alleys, and finally coming across a shop that specialised in Greek items. The next moment she was inside, inspecting, bargaining, and finally securing. When she left the shop her debt had grown substantially.

She was looking forward to showing her bargains to Marco, but so far there was no word from him, and that evening the two women dined alone. Later, as they sat together over coffee, Lucia suddenly said, 'Perhaps we should speak of what is on our minds. My dear, does it seem very terrible to you that I'm seeking a suitable wife for my son?'

'A little odd perhaps. Doesn't Marco mind the idea of marrying a stranger?'

'That's the worst of it, he doesn't mind at all. He was engaged once but it came to an end. Since then he's acted as though emotion was nothing but a stage in life that he'd put behind him and was relieved to have done so.'

'Did he love her?'

'I believe so, but he's never spoken about it. He slammed a door on the subject and nobody is allowed past, even me. Perhaps I'm a sentimental fool, but I loved Etta so much, and she died far too young. If I could see our families united in marriage and then in children, that's all I could ask for.'

'I wish you'd tell me about her.'

'I was friends with one of her sisters, who took me home to meet the family. Etta was ten years older than me, but she took me under her wing, for my mother was dead. I was a bridesmaid at her wedding, and one of the first people to see your father when he was born.

'We wanted our sons to grow up together, but I married late, and then it was years before Marco was born, so it didn't happen. And then my darling Etta died, and I still miss her so much. She was the only person I could confide in. Men aren't the same.'

'Am I really like her?'

For answer Lucia opened a cupboard and pulled out a photo album.

'There!' she said, opening it at an early page. 'That's Etta when she was your age.'

The young woman in the picture was dressed in the fashion of fifty years earlier, and her face was the one Harriet saw in her own mirror.

'I really am her granddaughter,' Harriet said, in a slow, wondering voice.

'Much more than Olympia,' Lucia confirmed. 'She would have been quite unsuitable. A sweet girl but an airhead, although, of course, I thought of her first because I'd known her for years. I wish I'd known you better. If only your mother hadn't kept you from us!'

'If only—*what?*'

'Your father said she wanted nothing to do with any of us after the split. She insisted on going home to England and raising you to be English.' She was looking at Harriet's face. 'Isn't that true?'

'No,' Harriet seethed, 'it most certainly isn't. He forced her to go back to England and just shut us out.'

'That woman!' Lucia said at once. 'He's always been in thrall to her. I never liked your father. He's a spineless weakling and quite unworthy of his mother. Now I'm totally disgusted with him.'

'So am I,' Harriet fumed. 'He denied me my Italian heritage.'

'Well, now you can claim it back again,' Lucia said warmly.

'Yes,' Harriet mused. 'I can.'

'Would it be tactless of me to suggest that you start by dressing in our country's fashion?'

'You mean my clothes look as if I bought them second-hand?' Harriet asked bluntly.

'Of course not. But among the many English talents *haute couture* is not perhaps—' she left the sentence delicately unfinished.

'No, it's not,' Harriet said decisively. 'You're right. It's time I started being who I am.' Then her confidence wavered. 'Whoever that is,' she added uncertainly.

'Never say such a thing again,' Lucia commanded. 'From this moment, you start life again.'

Next morning they went to the Via dei Condotti, the most exclusive shop in Rome. There Lucia cast a critical eye over the parade of garments, loftily dismissing this one, ordering that one set aside.

Slowly the pile of clothes grew, some to be taken as they were, some to be altered. The total wipe out of her wardrobe gave Harriet the feeling of being another person. It was strange, but she liked it.

Then she was introduced to Signora Talli, an ultra-fashionable modiste who spent a whole afternoon studying her face and redesigning it. Harriet had barely bothered with make-up. A touch of lipstick, a hint of eye shadow, and who needed more? That was her philosophy. She was soon shown the error of her ways.

Her eyes—such a magnificent shade of green, they must be highlighted, made larger—'How?' she asked nervously. The colour of the lipstick must be balanced with the colour of the eyes. Apparently any shade other than the one she normally wore would be preferable. She relapsed into cowed silence, convinced that she'd stumbled onto a branch of the higher science.

At last everything was in place. The woman who looked back at her from the mirror was a stranger with enormous, shadowy eyes and a mouth whose width had been cleverly emphasised. She herself had always tried to minimise that width.

Then Signora Talli took up a pair of scissors.

'Not my hair,' Harriet said, alarmed.

'Your face needs to be seen,' Lucia explained. 'You can't hide it behind that curtain.'

But Harriet, so pliable until then, became suddenly stubborn, inexplicably dismayed by the thought of losing her mane. The other two finally yielded, but insisted that she wear it up. In a few moments her long hair was piled high, altering the whole shape of her head, and revealing an exquisitely long, slender neck that she'd almost forgotten that she had. She surveyed herself, torn between dismay and a tingle of excitement. Unbidden the thought came into her mind that she would enjoy Marco's surprise when he saw her.

They finally selected six garments, five to be altered and delivered by the following day, and one, an olive-green trouser suit and satin shirt, that they took home with them. Harriet could see that it suited her perfectly, and when she sat down to supper with Lucia she felt good. Marco too, she thought, would approve if he happened to walk in now.

But the evening passed with no sign of him, and no word. Lucia called his mobile phone and growled with displeasure at finding herself talking to a machine.

'No, I will not leave a message,' she snapped.

'He's very busy,' Harriet placated her, although in truth she too felt like snapping.

'It's been several days. So he's busy. He can't spare some time for his—his—?'

'But I'm not his anything,' Harriet said quickly. 'I'm only here so that Marco and I can get to know each other.'

Lucia gave her a speaking glance. 'Well, you're certainly getting to know my son. Selfish, blinkered, indifferent.'

It seemed to be true. Was this really Marco's idea of courtship, to leave her here to win his mother's good will, as though that was the only thing that mattered?

By the time they went to bed neither woman was in a good mood.

The rest of the clothes arrived next day at the end of the afternoon, and Lucia made her parade in them while she surveyed her critically.

'I'm not sure about this evening dress,' Harriet said. 'It's tight.'

'And why not? You have the figure for it. It shows off your curves admirably.'

Harriet twisted before the mirror. 'I don't have cur—goodness, yes I do.'

She turned around, trying to see as much of the saffron satin as possible, without being too alarmed at the way it revealed her figure.

'Hmm!' she said, beginning to feel good.

'You should have bought yourself decent clothes before, instead of wasting your time on ancient history. Dead men are all very well in their way, but they don't wolf whistle.'

'Maybe I don't want to be wolf whistled.'

'Are you a woman or not? You have a splendid bust. You should show it off.'

'I am showing it off,' she said, tugging at the bosom in a vain attempt to get it higher. 'Lots of it. Oh, dear! This satin is so tight that you can tell I'm not wearing anything underneath.'

'Good. Excellent. *Marco, my dear boy!*'

Startled, Harriet swung around to see that Marco had come quietly into the room and was watching them with pleasure. Lucia rose and gave him an embrace which he returned affectionately before dropping a kiss onto Harriet's cheek. His aftershave reached her faintly, tangy, sharp, intensely masculine.

She wondered if he'd heard what she said about being naked under the dress. Or did he just know anyway? She wished she could stop being so conscious of her own body with only the thin satin to protect it. She resisted the temptation to tug again at the material over her bosom. She had the sensation that Marco was looking at the swell of her breasts; which was nonsense, because he wasn't even facing in her direction.

'Don't you think Harriet is improved?' Lucia demanded robustly.

'I think she's very beautiful,' Marco agreed. 'But her hair should be up.'

'I agree,' Lucia said. 'Etta, why haven't you put it up today? It looked so nice.' She seized a handful of hair and swept it up onto Harriet's head.

Startled, Harriet said, 'No,' sharply, and pulled it down again. It covered her exposed bosom a little, but there was another reason, that she couldn't understand.

She began to turn away but Marco's hands were on her shoulders, bringing her around to face him. Then she felt his fingers on her neck, twining in her hair, drawing it up and back.

'Why do you want to hide your face?' he asked.

'That's not what I—'

'I think it is.' He looked at her for a moment before saying gently, 'I also think your father has a lot to answer for.'

'I don't know what you—' The words died on her lips. Hearing it put into words she knew exactly what he meant.

'Just because your face didn't please him, you think it won't please any man,' Marco said. 'And you're wrong.'

She was stunned at the sudden revelation. That early rejection that she'd believed she could cope with, had marked her to this day. And this cool, unemotional man had been the one to see the truth in her heart.

She met his eyes. Then she drew in a sharp breath and became still as she saw something in them—or had she? It was gone so fast that it might have been an illusion.

'Put it up,' he said abruptly. 'Long hair is all wrong with that dress.'

The prosaic reason brought her back down to earth. She hurried away to her room to find the woman Lucia had deputed to act as her maid, and who swirled her hair into the exquisite creation of the previous day.

When she went down Marco put a glass of wine in her hand. He didn't mention her appearance but he smiled and gave a brief nod of pleasure. Lucia had recovered from her joy at the sight of her son and remembered that she was displeased with him.

'I suppose we should feel grateful that you've deigned to remember us at last,' she said caustically. 'Do we get five minutes of your precious time, or ten?'

'Don't be angry with me, Mamma,' he said, laughing. 'I've come to make amends by taking Harriet out tonight.'

CHAPTER FOUR

BELLA FIGURA was a nightclub on the Via Veneto, a few yards along from Marco's apartment. It was hidden away in the depths of the building, and as soon as they arrived Harriet could sense the atmosphere; sophisticated, knowing, and above all discreet. She wondered how many women Marco had brought here, and how many notes had changed hands with close-mouthed doormen.

He led her to a table near the stage, yet sufficiently to one side to afford some privacy. The floorshow had not started waiters hurried to and fro, taking orders. Marco summoned one of them with a look, which annoyed several customers who'd been waiting longer. He seemed not to notice.

As before he was an excellent host and she relaxed, even beginning to feel easier about the revealing dress.

'I'm sorry to have been so remiss,' he said. 'My mother is very annoyed with me. Are you?'

'No,' she said, not entirely truthfully. 'You

must have been deluged with work after being away, although I daresay you travel with a laptop, and don't miss very much.'

He nodded. 'I have a good assistant, but I prefer to keep my own finger on the pulse. I'm grateful that you understand. I'm afraid my mother doesn't. She thinks you'll be offended and rush back to England.'

'No way,' she said cheerfully. 'I'm having a wonderful time. Your mother and I get on splendidly.'

'So I gather from her. By the way, did I imagine that I saw you in the Via Veneto yesterday?'

'No, I picked up a cab there after I'd done some shopping. I found a shop a couple of streets away—'

It all came tumbling out, her visit, the treasures she'd discovered, the difficulty of deciding which to buy, the moment of half-guilty indulgence, the thrill of possession. Marco listened to her, at first with a smile, then with growing alarm.

'What in heaven's name did you buy?'

She rattled of the list.

'And they cost *how much*?'

'They're bargains,' she defensively. 'They'll look wonderful in the shop.'

'The shop that's already up to its ears in debt.

Good grief woman, have you no sense of the value of money?'

'Look, I know money's important, I'm not saying it isn't.'

'Now there's a concession!' he said scathingly.

'But it isn't necessarily first on my list of priorities—'

'I'd be interested to know just where it does come on your list of priorities.'

She was annoyed into frankness. 'Pretty low when I'm negotiating for an object of beauty.'

'Beauty costs money,' he said bluntly.

'Oh, really!'

'All right, tell me I'm wrong.'

She couldn't. An antique dealer knew better than anyone how much beauty cost, and having to concede the point exasperated her more than anything.

'I've seen your accounts remember,' Marco said, 'and a more soul-destroying experience I don't recall. I think you see good business practice as a sort of optional extra.'

'Rubbish!'

'What did you say?'

'All right, I admit I tend to leave that kind of thing to take care of itself.'

He stared at her glassy eyed. *'You leave business to take care of itself?'*

'Well, you knew I was like that.'

'I didn't know you were going to be "like that" in Rome.'

'I'm like that everywhere,' she said defiantly.

'So I'm beginning to understand. Maybe I should have spelled it out that a condition of my loan was that you don't make your financial situation worse.'

'I haven't made it worse. That stuff will sell at a profit.'

'Always assuming that you can find "kind" homes for it? Of all the—look, you're a dealer. Don't you know better than to walk into another dealer's shop and buy at full price?'

'Of course I do, but I couldn't help myself.'

'*Maria vergine!* You couldn't help yourself. If I bought stock in Novamente instead of Kalmati I should like to see my clients' faces when Novamente collapsed and I explained that it wasn't my fault because I couldn't help myself.'

'That's different,' she said frostily.

'I don't see why. Let's all live on emotional impulse with no sense of responsibility. If you, why not me?'

'Because you wouldn't know how to live on emotional impulse.'

'Thank heavens!' he said fervently.

'I am *not* irresponsible. I know all this stuff—'

'It's not enough to know it. You have to live by it.'

'When I saw those pieces I fell in love with them. You don't understand that, do you?'

'Only too well. You fell in love and abandoned all common sense, all perspective, all objectivity. Never, never make a decision when you're in love, whether it's with an object or—' he checked himself. He was breathing rapidly.

The appearance of a waiter was a diversion, one that he was glad of, she thought. He didn't look at her as the plates from the first course were cleared away and the second course served, and when they were alone again he smiled as though the moment had never happened.

'I didn't bring you out to criticise you,' he said. 'Perhaps I went a little too far.'

'Just a little,' she agreed. 'I suppose to someone who operates in higher finance I must seem raving mad.'

'Don't let's start on that again,' he begged. 'But let me look at the paperwork. I can tell you how to—that is, I may be able to suggest things you might find useful.'

'Thank you,' she said meekly.

He seemed about to reply, then caught the gleam in her eyes and thought better of it.

'What exactly do you do?' she asked.

'I work for the Banco Orese Nationale. It's a merchant bank, and I deal in stocks and shares, advising clients, research into market trends.'

'Go on.'

He settled into an explanation that lasted well into the second course and Harriet listened with genuine interest.

'Control is the answer,' he said once. 'If you're not in control, somebody else is. So you must always be the one in control. If I'm trying to beat someone down on the price of stock I always make sure I have one piece of information more than he does. Then I'm in control. He may think he is but I know that I am.

'You lost control of your shop, and now I'm in control—no, don't get mad. I'm not getting at you. I'm just helping you to avoid predators like me in future.'

'It's OK, go on,' she said, too fascinated to take up the cudgels again. She lacked the killer instinct to put really tough business practises into action, but she could follow complicated financial arguments.

When Marco checked himself and said, 'Let me put that another way,' she answered indignantly.

'You don't have to talk down to me. I understand every word.'

'Well it's a damned sight more than your sister can,' he growled. 'What is it?'

She had burst out laughing. Now she choked and said, 'It was just the thought of you talking like this to Olympia, and her trying to look interested.'

He grinned. 'Her eyes were glazed. Come to think of it, most women's eyes glaze after the first minute.'

'I should think so, too. If you take someone out on a date she doesn't want to be lectured about market trends.'

'You didn't mind.'

'That's different. We're business partners.'

'So we are,' he said after a moment. 'And this is a board meeting.'

'To consider the project so far, and work out *modus operandi* for the next stage.'

'Well, as a start, can we agree that you'll curb your purchasing instinct for a while? I'd like some input in future.'

'You meant you want to stop me spending money?'

'I was trying to put it politely. The blunt version is that from now on I hold the purse-strings.'

She'd been feeling more kindly towards him

but that vanished abruptly. 'What did you say?' she asked with a sweetness that should have warned him.

'No more buying. *Basta!* Enough.'

'Because you say so?'

'Because I say so. I'm doing a complete overhaul of your financial arrangements and you do nothing more until I've got them on a sensible footing.'

'Well, well! What happened to tact?'

'To hell with tact. Tact will bankrupt you.'

'Bankrupt *you*, you mean?'

'Nonsense,' he said impatiently. 'It isn't in your power to bankrupt me.'

'How interesting! I really must marry you for your money. Let's announce the engagement at once.'

'What a proposition. Irresistible!'

'Well, let's face it, you haven't anything else to offer. You're rude, overbearing, dictatorial, arrogant—'

'Is that supposed to floor me? Think again. There's nothing wrong with arrogance if you're sure of your ground.'

'And I'll bet you're always sure of your ground.'

'Too right. It stops me being wrong-footed by people who don't know what they're talking about.'

'Meaning me?'

'Meaning anyone.'

'Meaning the entire rest of the world, as far as you're concerned. So now you'll have exactly the wife you need, someone who's seen the worst of you and will put up with it for the sake of your money.'

He grunted. 'You think you've seen the worst of me?'

'Well, I hope the rest isn't even more unpleasant.'

'It can be,' he said, his eyes glinting. 'It can be a lot more unpleasant. Think hard before taking me on.'

'Fine! It's all off. Here endeth the shortest engagement in history. The protagonists couldn't stand each other.'

She dropped her voice on the last words, aware that she was attracting attention. Marco also looked around, before lowering his voice and leaning closer to her.

'You're being melodramatic,' he said coldly. 'There's no need for all this emotionalism.'

She too leaned closer. 'I'm not being emotional, I'm being coldly realistic. Why not? It works for you.'

'You know nothing about me,' he snapped. 'All this because I want to organise your finances—'

'You don't want to "organise" my finances, you want to control them, and me. Where would it stop if I let you?'

'*Let* me? Do you think I'm asking permission?'

'I think you'd better be.'

'Harriet, I'm telling you, no more buying.'

'And I'm telling you that you've made me a loan, not bought me body and soul. The shop is mine.'

'For how long if I decided to turn really nasty?'

'You? Nasty? Surely not! Listen to me, Marco, I own that shop, I run it, and I alone decide what it needs. If I see stock I want, I won't ask you first, I'll buy it and tell them to bill me.'

'And if I insist on returning it?'

'That'll be hard because I'll be back in England.'

'Having smuggled an Etruscan necklace or two under your jacket, I suppose?' he said with heavy irony.

'It was a fake and I'll do whatever is necessary,' she said through gritted teeth.

'*Marco, my boy!*'

They both looked up quickly to see a large, middle-aged man who'd approached their table while they were preoccupied. Marco rose to shake his hand, introducing him to Harriet as Alfredo Orese.

Orese, she thought. And he worked for the Banca Orese Nationale.

'Unforgivable of me to interrupt two love-birds,' Alfredo said jovially, purloining a chair from another table and joining them. 'Nice to see a young couple absorbed in each other, head to head, oblivious to the world, know what I mean?'

That must be how they had looked, Harriet realised, smiling noncommittally.

'Not a word, Alfredo,' Marco said amiably. 'Let us keep our secrets.'

Alfredo put his finger over his lips and winked. He was somewhat the worse for wear, and seemed less like a banker than a man who liked a good time. He ordered a bottle of the best champagne, toasted them noisily, kissed Harriet's cheek and finally, to their relief, took himself off.

'I'm sorry about that,' Marco said, letting out his breath. 'He's a good fellow, means no harm.'

'And likes playing at being a banker,' she said wryly.

'How did you know?'

'The name. But I reckon the name is the only reason he's there.'

He grinned. 'Yes, but to his credit he understands that and doesn't interfere. You ought to marry him. He's got ten times what I have and he'd let you blow the lot without protest.'

'Ah, but he wouldn't give me a good fight like you do.'

'You can count on me for those.'

'All right, I'll grant you that my financial management leaves something to be desired—'

'I wouldn't myself have dignified your carry-on with the name of financial management—'

'Do you want to fight again?' she asked sweetly.

'No, it's too soon after the last time. Let's space them and get our breath back.'

'Will you be quiet while I make a sort of concession?'

He looked at her attentively.

'I admit I've made some mistakes—did you say something?'

'Not a word.'

'I've made a few mistakes, and I shall be *interested* to hear your advice.'

His lips twitched. 'Interested?'

'Interested.'

'To the point of taking it?'

'Let's see what the future holds.'

He grinned. Humour altered his face as though a light had come on inside him. He could be charming, she thought, when he allowed himself to relax. She was beginning to understand his habit of describing everything in business terms. They were the words he understood most easily, but they covered something else deep inside him, and she was beginning to be intrigued by what that 'something else' might be.

'Enough for tonight,' he said. 'It's a draw.'

She laughed and let it go.

As the coffee was being served the lights were lowered. Members of the band took their place on the low stage. A young woman came to the microphone and began to sing in a breathy voice. It was a song about loss and physical longing, the persistence of desire when all hope had gone.

'I feel you touching me—though we're apart—your hands, your lips are everywhere...'

She was a skilful artist, managing to squeeze the last ounce of sensuality from every word, every cunningly placed pause. A new atmosphere, romantic, delicate, subtly erotic, began to pervade the club.

By slow degrees Harriet felt herself come alive with the consciousness that she was sitting close to an attractive man, with only a thin layer of material between him and her nakedness. Suddenly the dress felt alarmingly low.

She stole a look at Marco to see if he was equally aware of her, but he was watching the stage. Her eyes were drawn to his hands, which were long and fine, but with a hint of power.

'Your hands touch me everywhere—' crooned the singer.

It was absurd to feel her body responding merely to a thought, but she couldn't control the warmth that was stealing over her. How would those hands touch a woman? How would it feel to be touched intimately by them? It was as though she already knew. She took a deep, shuddering breath and fixed her eyes on the floor.

For his part, Marco was directing his eyes to anywhere but her. He'd gone to his mother's villa tonight prepared only to stay for supper and depart, his duty done. One look at Harriet had changed his mind. Here was the sensual, flamboyant creature who'd hidden beneath her dowdy disguise, tantalising him with her elusiveness from the very first night.

His decision to take her out had been spur of the moment, something which shocked him but did not deter him. He kept a room at the villa and a set of evening clothes, so a change of plan presented no problems. As he drove her into Rome he'd wondered how the evening would go, what they would talk about. It hadn't occurred to him that they would fight, but now he thought perhaps it should have done.

Finally he stole a glance at her, and saw that her face was averted from the stage, slightly towards him, but not looking directly at him. He realised that she wasn't seeing anything external, but was lost in an inner world where he wasn't invited. It was absurd to feel jealous, but he wished she would notice him. She didn't.

The blue light from the stage drained all other colour from her, and sharply emphasised the shadows. For a moment she didn't look like a living woman but like the statue of some ancient queen, perhaps Nefertiti or Cleopatra: some great lady, statuesque, imperious, magnificent.

But he knew that this was only part of her. The next moment she could come alive with the mischievous laughter of a child, or glare at him with the fierceness of an adversary. There was no knowing.

He saw that Alfredo was attracting his attention from a few yards away and forced himself to smile. Alfredo was a good fellow, not the brightest, but amiable, and he would be useful in gaining a partnership. He was indicating Harriet, winking, making 'ho ho' gestures implying that they were both men of the world. Suddenly Marco wanted to knock him down.

The singer departed, amid applause and the band struck up for dancing.

'Would you care to take the floor?' Marco asked politely.

She took his hand and he led her onto the dance floor, which rapidly became too crowded to do more than shuffle. He held her firmly, close but not too close, and she found that her step fell in with his easily. The effect of the sultry song was still on her, driving out all thoughts except that she was enjoying this moment and anticipating the next one. She smiled.

'What is it?' he asked at once.

'I'm just having a good time.'

'That smile meant something.'

'It meant I'm having a good time.'

'No, more than that. Tell me.'

His insistence disturbed her. She met his eyes and saw in them something that was too intense for the trivial question. Then somebody collided with her and she felt Marco's hands tighten, steadying her. She was pressed against him, his face close to hers. Her senses swam and she closed her eyes to hide whatever they might have revealed to him.

'Look at me,' he murmured.

She did so and found him watching her intently. She could feel the movement of his thighs against hers, and the warmth of his hand in the small of her back, seeming to move with the flexing of her body, as though the material between had vanished. She was possessed by thoughts and sensations that shocked her with their frankness and urgency, and a little gasp broke from her.

'What is it?' he wanted to know.

'I—nothing—nothing—' she struggled to make sense. 'Just the heat.'

'Yes, the atmosphere is getting a little too much,' Marco agreed. 'My apartment is close by. Let me give you a coffee there.'

It was half past two when they emerged, and the stars were bright in the sky. Except for a few wanderers like themselves the street was deserted. Marco drew her hand through his arm and they strolled the short distance to the apartment block where he lived.

To Harriet's relief the walk and the night air calmed her down. By the time they'd taken the lift to the fifth floor she felt in control of herself again.

She was curious to see the place Marco called home. She'd tried to imagine it and been unable to. He was so impenetrable that it was impossible to conjure up anything that he hadn't chosen to reveal. Now she saw the truth, and at first it took her by surprise. Then she realised that it was exactly what she had subconsciously expected.

No home was ever more austere and unrevealing. The marble floors were honey-coloured, the walls white. The greatest splash of colour came from a dark red leather sofa. The lighting was concealed. Some modern pictures hung on the wall, and a few decorative pieces stood on the shelves. To Harriet's cursory glance they seemed excellent.

It was the home of a man who hid himself away, perhaps even from himself, she thought. There was a photograph of Lucia, but nothing else personally revealing. Through the open door to his bedroom Harriet could see a computer, a fax machine that was inching out paper at that moment, a range of telephones, and two television screens. This man took his work to bed.

Into her mind came Olympia saying, 'A lady-killer...you might say he ''loves 'em and leaves 'em'' except that he doesn't love 'em.'

Whatever happened in Marco's personal life, it happened there, in that large unadorned bed, in front of the technology that brought the world's stock markets to him at all hours.

'I'll make some coffee,' he called from the kitchen.

The kitchen was also austere, but beautiful,

its white relieved by copper and blue. He moved about it easily, like a man used to doing his own cooking, which figured, she thought. Even a small prosaic action, like making coffee, he performed perfectly.

'Delicious,' she said, sipping with relish. 'You have a beautiful home.'

'Thank you. Not everyone likes it.'

'It's peaceful, I like that a lot. And you know how to show off your art pieces to advantage. The plain background does a lot for them, and the way you've arranged the lighting.'

'Thank you. Praise from you is praise indeed. Would you like to give me your opinion of my collection?'

She finished her coffee before approaching a vase on its own plinth. It was oddly flamboyant against the austere background, and she correctly assessed it as French fifteenth century. 'And it's genuine.'

'Everything in my collection is real,' he said firmly.

She smiled, replacing the vase on its plinth and moving away. 'Let's not argue about that.'

'I agree,' he said, standing before her. 'Arguing is a waste of time.'

Very deliberately he leaned forward, placed one hand behind her head, and drew her towards him. His lips touched hers lightly, cautiously, feeling his way before taking the next step. He evidently decided that the signs were favourable for he increased the pressure of his mouth on hers.

The sensation was pleasant, and Harriet let herself go with it, enjoying the cool ease with which he took possession. He acted as though there was all the time in the world for them to explore each other, and she found this relaxing. When his arm curved about her waist she moved in easily, slipping her own arms about him, letting her hands enjoy the sensation of whipcord strength that came through his elegant evening clothes.

He felt good, not bulky and muscular, but lean and hard, with a concealed strength that pleased her. But everything about Marco was just right, most of all his embrace. He was as smooth and expert at this as at every other social skill. He would know just the moment to deepen the kiss and increase their mutual excitement. She waited, but the pressure on her lips eased and she had a sudden view of his face and it troubled her.

Harriet stirred, feeling strangely disturbed. Her body was responding but her mind was growing tense. Something about this wasn't right. She put up her hands to push Marco away but he resisted, moving his mouth slowly over hers in a way that bid her leave everything to him. There was nothing for her to do but be acquiescent.

Like blazes!

She tightened her hands on his shoulders in a way that he couldn't mistake. 'That's enough,' she said firmly and stepped away, freeing herself. 'You've got a nerve, you really have!'

'For pity's sake!' he said, exasperated. 'This is the twenty-first century, not the nineteenth. You couldn't have thought I was just going to hold your hand. We've spent a delightful evening together, we've danced and held each other close, and you say you didn't expect me to kiss you?'

'You weren't kissing me,' she said in a shaking voice. 'You were damned well inspecting the property.'

'What?'

'You know what I mean. That wasn't a kiss, it was a survey to see if a takeover would be in your interests.'

'Now you're being foolish.'

'I could hear your mind ticking away,' she said furiously. 'Test the ground, so far and no further. You wouldn't want me to get any ideas before you've made your own mind up in case I was a nuisance afterwards, you cold, calculating—'

'Don't say any more,' he snapped. 'I get the picture. I just wish I knew what it is you want.'

'It's very simple. If you're going to kiss me, do it properly, not—'

She never got to say the last words. Her mouth was silenced by another mouth descending fiercely onto it. She didn't recall how she came to be in his arms, but there they were about her, holding her still while his lips worked over hers with skill and determination. She tried to protest about the way he was using her, but he muttered, 'Shut up! You said this was what you wanted, and it's what you're going to have.'

She didn't try to argue further. This was a very angry man, giving a very angry kiss, and how could she complain when she'd brought it on herself? But she found she didn't want to complain. An excitement she'd never known before was running through her like wildfire. It wasn't the soft, sensual thrumming that had pervaded her in the club, but a heady, intoxicating thrill that caught her unaware. She couldn't think, she could only feel, and yearn, and reach for him.

His hands were beginning to wander over her, feeling her small waist, flaring out to discover the smooth satin curve of her behind. There they lingered as though relishing the discovery, before reaching the zip at the centre and inching upwards to the hook at the top. A few more movements and the zip would come down, leaving her nearly naked in his arms. How long would it take him then to have the dress off her, and what would she do? She knew she must decide quickly but it was hard because her body was tense with delight, driving everything out of her head.

She could sense that he was drawing her to the bedroom, past the point of no return. It mustn't happen like this, when they were half hostile, but she couldn't think how else it might happen. The undercurrent of hostility was often there, she realised, giving spice and surprise to their relationship. Her urgency increased.

The buzz was so faint that she almost didn't hear it. She tried to blot it out, but Marco was already disengaging himself from her. He made a sound of annoyance at the interruption, but he disengaged himself nonetheless.

Dreamily she watched as he snatched up the phone and she waited for him to put the caller off. Instead he tensed, alert.

'Yes,' he barked into the phone. 'This is Marco Calvani—go on—'

Harriet stared, stunned by how quickly he'd switched his attention, as though he hadn't really been involved at all. But she couldn't believe that, not while she could still feel the heat from his nearness and the driving force of his mouth.

At last Marco took the phone from his ear, but he didn't hang up.

'I'm sorry, but this is important,' he told her. 'I won't be able to drive you home, but there's an excellent cab firm—the number's in that book.'

'Wh-what?' she asked, dazed.

'Just there on the table beside you—hello!' He'd turned back to the phone. 'Yes, I'm still here. Let's talk.'

'And you know what really made me mad,' she told an outraged Lucia later that night. *'He even left me to call my own cab.'*

CHAPTER FIVE

THE following day a delicate bouquet was delivered to the villa, with a beautifully worded note from Marco, regretting that their delightful evening had been 'so unfortunately cut short'. Harriet passed it to Lucia, who expressed her own opinion with a sound of disgust, but mercifully didn't ask Harriet any questions. Her manner was that of a woman biding her time.

After two days Marco telephoned, inviting them both to lunch at the bank. The Orese Nationale had a private restaurant where the top levels of the hierarchy dined in exclusive grandeur, and where they entertained their most important guests. The two women were treated like queens, by Marco and some of his colleagues.

Lucia had been here three times before, but she was the only woman Marco had ever invited, until now. Harriet understood the implication, that none of his passing relationships had been so honoured. She'd meant to protest about his unchivalrous behaviour after the nightclub, but it was impossible in these circumstances. Lucia too was silenced, which might, she thought cynically, have been Marco's idea.

Alfredo Orese couldn't keep a secret, and the news was soon all over Rome that Marco had been seen at the nightclub with a new woman. But this one was different. She was staying with his mother, and she had dined at the bank. After that speculation raged, and came to more or less the right conclusion.

'So now your engagement isn't a secret,' Lucia said with satisfaction some days later. They were sitting at breakfast, Marco having arrived late the night before, and slept over.

Harriet looked at her quickly. 'It isn't precisely an engagement,' she said.

'Then what is it, precisely?'

She looked at Marco but he gave her no help, and she floundered, 'It's sort of—unofficial.'

'I have no patience with all this shilly-shallying. Anyone can see that you're right for each other, and now the world knows you're engaged.'

'You wouldn't have given them that impression by any chance?' Marco demanded ironically.

'I didn't need to. Everyone saw you lost in each other at *Bella Figura*.'

Since they could hardly explain that they'd been fighting at the time neither of them answered, and Lucia took this for confirmation.

'And taking us to the bank was practically an announcement,' Lucia added. 'So now we must have a party. Everyone will expect it. They'll also expect a ring. See to it.' She bustled away before they could answer.

'What are we going to do?' Harriet demanded.

'A party's actually a good idea,' Marco said. 'It's time you met some family friends.'

'But an engagement party—a ring—'

'It changes nothing. We get engaged, we change our minds, we get unengaged. And my mother's right about the ring.' He scribbled an address and gave it to her. 'That's the best jeweller in Rome. I'll tell them to expect you.'

'You're not coming with me?'

'I have urgent business to attend to,' he said, not meeting her eye. 'They'll have a fine selection ready for you. Pick the best.'

She attended the jeweller later that day. He treated Signor Calvani's fiancée with awed respect, and showed her a selection of diamond rings, all of which looked lavish and frighteningly expensive. There was one that pleased her, a band of tiny diamonds set in white gold, crowned with one large diamond of marvellous quality. But she knew too much about jewellery not to guess its fabulous price, and there was no way she could accept it.

'Don't you have something a little—smaller,' she asked, feeling that 'cheaper' might be tactless.

'These are the ones Signor Calvani selected,' the jeweller said.

So he'd been to the shop. But not with her. Worse, he was trying to control her choice, and up with that she would not put.

'I'd like to see something else,' she said firmly.

He was aghast. 'But Signor Calvani—'

'Will not be wearing this ring. I will.'

'But—'

'Of course, if it's too much trouble, I can go elsewhere.'

Defeated, the little man produced a tray of less extravagant rings. Then he mopped his brow.

She finally chose a charming solitaire, resisting his attempts to direct her back to the luxury rings, and went away with it on her finger.

Marco arrived at the villa that evening, bearing a large black jeweller's box.

Harriet hadn't expected him to give in easily, and reckoned she didn't have to be clairvoyant to guess that the box contained the rings she'd rejected.

So it was war then! She was ready for him.

Marco greeted his mother pleasantly before taking Harriet aside.

'Thank you for my lovely ring,' she said, holding up her hand.

He took her hand between his and firmly removed the solitaire without even looking at it.

'Hey, what are you doing?'

'There was a mistake. He must have shown you the wrong tray.'

'There was no mistake. This was the one I liked.'

'My fiancée does not wear cheap rings,' Marco said firmly.

'Cheap? It must be worth ten thousand euros.'

'Exactly,' he said in a clipped voice. It was clear that he was keeping his annoyance under control.

'I see. If "your fiancée" was seen flaunting a mere ten grand your clients would start checking the value of their stocks and shares, to see if you were losing your financial touch.'

'Since you obviously understand I don't see why we're having this discussion.'

'Please give me back that ring.'

'No.'

'It's the one I want.'

There was a silence in which he raised his clenched hands to his head in a gesture that was an odd combination of frustration, obstinacy and helplessness. Their eyes met, determination on both sides. Marco opened the box.

'I would prefer you to select one of these,' he said, speaking carefully.

'And I would prefer the one I chose.'

Through gritted teeth he demanded, 'Why must everything be an argument?'

'Because you try to control me at every turn, and I won't have it.'

'Nonsense. I'm merely asking you to do what's proper to our situation. Good grief, Harriet, just the other day you spent more than this without turning a hair. Money I hadn't authorised, let me remind you.'

'Are we going to start that again?'

'I just think it odd that you'll plunder my pockets with the ruthlessness of a corporate raider when it's a question of an old carved stone, but over this you suddenly get delicate about the price. Where's the logic?'

'Who says there has to be logic?'

'It helps sometimes,' he said savagely.

'Then how's this for logic? It's not the price. It's you directing me here and there like a train running on rails. This train is coming off the rails and going her own way.'

'And never mind how it affects me?'

'Your clients will get over it.'

But he was cleverer than she had allowed for, and the next moment he come up with the one thing she wasn't prepared for. The anger died out of his face, and he looked at her with a rueful smile.

'Harriet, for a brilliant woman you can be remarkably stupid.'

'What does that mean?' she asked cautiously, divining a trap but unable to see where it lay.

'It's not my clients I'm afraid of. It's my mother.'

'Oh, really! If you're trying to persuade me that you're afraid of your mother—!'

'Terrified. What do think she's going to say to me if she thinks I've treated you shabbily over the ring?'

He was smiling at her in a way she found disturbing.

'I'll explain to her that this way my choice—'

'It's no good,' he sighed. 'She'll say I should have asserted myself. She doesn't know how hard that is with you. If you won't help me out I'll—well, I just don't know what I'll do.'

'Now you stop that,' she said severely, trying

not to respond to his smile. 'I see right through you, d'you hear?'

'I'm sure you do.'

'And you don't care a rap, do you, as long as you get your own way?'

'You understand me perfectly.'

'Well, of all the admissions—! You ought to be ashamed of yourself.'

'Why? Nothing wrong in getting your own way. Don't you like to do that?'

'Of course, but I have some scruples how I go about it.'

'Scruples are a waste of time,' he said seriously. 'If it works for you, go for it.'

'No matter who else—?'

'No matter anything.'

'But that's dreadful.'

'No, it makes sense and it gets things done. Now, why don't you just try this on?'

As he spoke he was slipping onto her finger the white gold ring that had drawn her attention in the shop. And he knew, of course. The jeweller had told him that this one had made her waver. At every turn he was there before her, and she must fight him.

But indignation faded in the beauty of the diamond band with its crown of one perfect jewel. She stretched out her hand to watch the light winking off the great stone, awed by its sheer extravagant glory.

'I can't take it,' she said desperately. 'I just can't.' But she didn't lower her hand.

'Mamma!' Marco hailed his mother, hovering eagerly in the doorway. 'Come and congratulate us on our engagement.'

As he spoke he held up Harriet's hand and Lucia gave a cry of admiration. 'Oh, *cara*, what a beautiful ring!'

'Yes, isn't it?' she said, regarding her betrothed with cynical eyes. There was no turning back now.

'How they'll all gasp when they see it!' Lucia exclaimed. 'Now we can really settle down to enjoy planning the party.'

'I shall have to be out of town for a few days,' Marco said instantly.

'Go away then,' his mother told him. 'We'll do much better without you.'

She departed, humming.

'I won't say anything about your total lack of scruples,' Harriet said, 'because we've already covered that. But I want it clearly understood that if I don't go through with this—and right now that seems very unlikely—you will take this ring back.'

'Naturally,' he said, shocked. 'You don't

think I'd have let you keep it? I'd need it for next time.'

His eyes were teasing her, and suddenly she didn't mind very much after all. He was overbearing and impossible, but there was nothing to be done about that. And he had a certain sly charm that could sneak in under her radar.

But there was something else, that she hardly dared admit to herself. Sensible Harriet was retreating into the shadows, banished by another Harriet who wanted to take risks and live life to the full: as long as it was with him.

The realisation shook her. She needed time to think about it.

By the end of supper Lucia and Marco had agreed a guest list. Looking over it Harriet saw a name that made her eyes light up. 'Baron Orazio Manelli,' she said excitedly.

'Do you know him?' Marco asked.

'No, but I want to. I've been trying to get past his front door for ages.'

'I suppose he has some antique that you want?'

'A thousand antiques, and from what I hear a lot of them have never been properly catalogued. He won't let anyone near them. But it'll be different now.' Her voice became casual. 'Do you know him well?'

'Well enough to get you past his front door. I gather that's what I'm expected to do?'

'It's not a problem is it?'

'Would it make any difference if it was?'

'Well—'

'Don't bother being polite. I'm glad to be of use.'

That was one hurdle cleared, she thought, glad that Marco seemed merely amused. A happy vista of unexplored treasures was opening up to her.

Marco was away for a week. Harriet and Lucia spent the time in a flurry of activity. Every one of the villa's army of servants was engaged in spring cleaning the place and bringing it to new life. A stream of invitations went out, including one to Harriet's father, but since there was no reply it seemed that he was still away.

Within a day a stream of acceptances started to come in. All society was agog to see the woman who had 'conquered the conqueror', a phrase that was repeated through the salons of the city until it reached Harriet's ears.

'Well, this is Rome after all,' she said wryly to Lucia. 'The perfect place for going into the lion's den.'

'Don't worry,' Lucia told her. 'Marco knows

all about the lions. He won't let you face them alone.'

Two days before the party Marco appeared at the villa and the three of them had a cheerful supper. Over coffee Lucia said, 'The family will start to arrive tomorrow. Are you ready to meet them?'

'A bit nervous,' Harriet admitted.

Lucia sighed. 'I'm a little nervous myself. Francesco is bringing Liza—I can hardly bring myself to call her his fiancée. It's an absurd name for a woman in her sixties.'

'It's not his fault they've left it so long,' Marco pointed out. 'He's been begging her to marry him for years, but since she was his housekeeper she had the strange idea that their marriage was inappropriate.'

Lucia sniffed. 'She was correct.'

Marco added, 'Harriet has already met Dulcie, Mamma.'

'It wouldn't surprise me to learn that Dulcie came into Harriet's shop to sell the family silver,' Lucia observed with some asperity.

'It was a marble horse head actually,' Harriet murmured without thinking. To cover this gaffe she added quickly, 'I really look forward to seeing her again. We got on very well. After we'd done business we'd have lunch together. She's great fun.'

Lucia blenched. 'Fun? Is that her only qual-
ification for being the future Contessa Calvani?'

'Well I—'

'Don't try to answer that,' Marco told her
quietly. 'Mamma, you're not being fair to
Harriet.'

'No, of course I'm not. It isn't your fault, my
dear.' She patted Harriet's hand and the moment mercifully passed.

'Leo, of course, won't arrive until the last
moment,' Lucia continued. 'He's uncomfortable
in society, or anywhere civilised.'

'True,' Marco said with a grin. 'In fact he
probably wouldn't come at all if he wasn't going on to America, and Rome Airport will give
him a more direct flight to Texas.'

'Texas!' Lucia sniffed again. 'Anyone would
think he was a cowboy.'

'Since he's going to a rodeo I suppose that's
what he is,' Marco said mildly.

'A rodeo?' Harriet echoed.

'Leo breeds horses in Tuscany,' Marco explained. 'They're fine animals and much in demand. He'll be riding in this rodeo and making
some sales, I dare say.'

'A cowboy!' Lucia sighed in despair. 'And
he should be Francesco's heir!'

Next morning she and Lucia were waiting at
the station for the Venice train, from which

Count Francesco Calvani appeared, on his arm a thin elderly woman. This was Liza, his promised bride, and the sight of them together made Harriet smile. Their secret love had lasted all these years, and now that it could flower openly their pride and joy in each other was touching. How many young couples would still feel that way after years, she wondered? Certainly not herself and Marco, who didn't even start with love.

Of course, he might well be right, and a sensible arrangement was the best thing. But there was a lump in her throat as she regarded the elderly lovers.

Marco's cousin Guido was a good-looking charmer with a wicked glint in his eyes. But mostly those eyes rested on Dulcie, who would become his bride in a few weeks. If ever a man was in love—! Harriet thought, liking him for it.

Dulcie greeted her with a whoop and an embrace. 'I can't believe it's really you. Just fancy, we're going to be related. That'll be great.'

'Yes,' Harriet agreed, wondering if that day would really come. The glittering ring on her finger was real enough but everything else had an air of unreality. For the moment the only thing to do was plunge into the festivities wholeheartedly, and she was eager to enjoy them, despite her many confusions.

She might disapprove of the count's marriage but Lucia's behaviour to Liza was charming. Behind her pride her heart was kind, and Liza was soon relaxing in her company.

She was also relaxed with Marco, Harriet noticed, evidently feeling that his kindness too could be relied on. He kissed her cheek, addressed her as Aunt, and gave her his arm into the house.

Over supper Guido entertained them with the story of the many misunderstandings that had attended his first meeting with Dulcie, in Venice, when she'd thought he was a gondolier, and he hadn't known that she was hiding a secret of her own. They were all laughing when Harriet looked up and saw a tall, massively built young man standing in the doorway. With his shaggy hair and rough-hewn appearance he was immediately identifiable as the 'country bumpkin'.

There was a general cry of '*Leo!*', and Guido and Marco rose to shake his hand and thump him on the back. The young giant grinned and thumped them back, then kissed Lucia and Dulcie. Harriet got to her feet to meet him, and he gave her the appraising glance she was growing used to. He was as handsome as the other two, but the impression he made was more powerfully physical. The Calvani men, Harriet decided, were simply too much.

She instinctively liked Leo, who shook her hand and kissed her cheek with the simplicity of a man who found actions easier than thought. Keeping her hand between his, he then looked her up and down with an appreciative grin that went on getting broader. Playing up to him, she gazed back, until Marco coughed significantly.

'Who are you?' she asked, giving him a dazed stare.

Everyone roared with laughter, including, she was glad to notice, Marco. He wasn't a man who would normally accept such teasing, but the family's appreciation of her quick wit had delighted him.

'Go away, Leo, while I remind my fiancée who I am,' Marco said with a grin. 'And leave her alone in future.'

Leo winked at her and hissed, 'The terrace at midnight,' in a stage whisper, but Harriet was prevented from answering by Marco's arm, firmly about her waist, drawing her away.

'We were just fooling,' she protested, still chuckling.

'I know, but you want to watch Leo. He "fools" with a lot of girls. He's a "love 'em and leave 'em" man.'

'Strange, I heard the same about you.'

His brows contracted. 'I wonder where you heard that.'

'Everywhere.' Her eyes challenged him and he backed down first.

'Let's finish supper,' he said.

Since the meal was half over Leo had a lot of catching up to do, and tucked in with gusto while the talk swirled around him. When he spoke it was usually to ask Harriet about herself, not pretending to be amorous now, but with every appearance of cousinly interest. It might have been simply good manners, but it warmed her heart. She began to feel as though a dream had come true against all the odds. This was the culmination of something that had been happening ever since Lucia had welcomed her at the station. She was accepted. The whole dashing, colourful Calvani family had opened its collective arms to her. To someone who'd felt rejected most of her life it was overwhelming.

It was hard to believe that the Calvani men came from the same family, their looks were so different, although they were all, as Lucia had observed to Harriet, 'handsome as devils'.

At seventy-two the count bore the marks of a lifetime's self-indulgence, but not enough to obliterate the remains of brilliant good looks.

Leo and Guido were half-brothers, Leo radiating the vigour and energy of a man of the earth: lusty, uncomplicated, great-hearted. Guido's build was slighter than his brother's, his boyish looks balanced by a shrewd intelligence, and he had a nervous energy that kept him restless, except when Dulcie was nearby.

To Harriet's eyes Marco was by far the most impressive, elegant, controlled, unrevealing, his own man in everything. In the heart of his family he was a changed man, relaxed, readier to laugh. But it was still hard to imagine him behaving with Leo's cheerful indifference, or regarding a woman with the blatant adoration that shone from Guido's eyes.

She wondered about the woman he'd nearly married, and whose name was never mentioned in this house. Had he truly loved her, or had she fled him in despair at being unable to penetrate his protective shell? That was more likely, she thought.

And yet he had a surprise for her as the party broke up to go to bed, taking her hand and leading her out onto the terrace.

'You have a midnight appointment out here,' he reminded her.

'But not with you,' she said provocatively.

'It had better be with me,' he said with a smile that provoked her even more.

And she wanted nothing better, she thought as his lips touched hers. There was a sweetness in this kiss that melted her and made her lean in to him, wanting more. But he drew back a little, and she saw him regarding her with an odd little half-smile. She raised her eyebrows in a query, but he only shook his head, and she felt the brief interlude had posed more questions than it answered.

On the night of the party Harriet was just finishing dressing when Dulcie, a dream in dark blue silk and diamonds, swept into her room.

'Wow!' she exclaimed. 'You look fantastic. No wonder you melted the Iceman's heart.'

'The Iceman?'

'I shouldn't have said that,' Dulcie was conscience stricken. 'But Guido says it's what the family have always called him. Not to his face, naturally. You know how grim he can be. But of course you see a side of him that nobody else does.' She gave a delighted chuckle. 'Now I've made you blush.'

'I'm not,' Harriet said, although conscious that she was going pink. There was something in the implication that she and Marco were lovers that discomposed her. To hide her face she turned away and patted down her dress.

The beautician had come out from the salon

to take charge of her appearance, and Harriet's face was made-up with subtle flattery, so that her expressive green eyes dominated her face. Her hair was swept up on top of her head, with just a few curving wisps gently drifting down about her cheeks and neck.

She wore a clinging dress of golden brown crushed velvet. She knew she looked good and the knowledge gave her confidence.

There was a knock at the door and Dulcie opened it to reveal Guido and Marco, both in bow-ties and dinner jackets, both incredibly handsome.

Marco surveyed Harriet with satisfaction. '*Bene!* Just as I hoped. This will look splendid on you.'

He opened a black box, revealing a heavy gold chain. Dulcie stared at it, wide-eyed, before seizing Guido's hand and whisking him away.

'Spoilsport,' her beloved chided her when they were out in the corridor. 'It would have been fun to see the Iceman playing the lover.'

'You wouldn't have seen it,' Dulcie told him. 'Marco wouldn't open up with us there. But now that we're gone I'll bet they're locked in a passionate embrace.'

Guido inched hopefully back towards the door. 'Can't we just—?'

'Behave yourself! Besides, I have other plans for you.'

His eyes gleamed. 'Ah, that's different.' He allowed himself to be led away in the opposite direction.

They would both have been disappointed had they seen Marco's calm demeanour as he raised the elaborate chain and draped it around Harriet's neck.

'I've always known that gold would suit you,' he said, fastening the clasp at the back. 'I was right.'

Awed, Harriet gazed at the woman in the mirror and didn't know her. This wasn't herself, but a magnificent creature, with a timeless splendour. She might have been Cleopatra, or some ancient pagan goddess. Marco had judged perfectly.

'Thank you,' she said. 'I never dreamed I could look like that.'

'I know. You have discerning eyes for everyone but yourself. I have known this about you from the first moment.'

A special note in his voice made her conscious that his fingers were still resting against her neck. Glancing in the mirror she met his eyes and saw in them a glow that he'd never shown her face to face. Then he seemed to become self-conscious, and the shutters came down again.

'Are you ready?' Lucia asked from the door. 'People are beginning to arrive.'

The other five were waiting in the corridor. Even Leo had managed to shrug himself into a dinner jacket. Lucia, splendid in rubies, surveyed them all with satisfaction.

'The Calvanis are a handsome family,' she said. 'And they attract handsome women. Now let's all go down and *knock 'em dead.*'

CHAPTER SIX

STANDING in the receiving line Harriet thought the guests would go on forever. There were a number of banking 'big names' and some of Marco's most important clients, but there were also a lot of titles, Countess this, Princess that, Duke, Baron. This was society with a capital S.

Where it wasn't titled, it was wealthy. Harriet guessed that half the bank vaults in Rome must have disgorged their contents of family jewels. Tiaras, *rivières*, bracelets, earrings, diamonds, rubies, emeralds and pearls, each one signifying that its wearer would compete in riches with any other woman there.

As she could herself, she realised. The glowing gold that Marco had fastened around her neck was, in itself, a declaration. And so was the ring. She shuddered at the thought of wearing a ring worth a 'mere' ten thousand in this company. The one now weighing down her hand informed the world that Marco Calvani's chosen bride was a woman who commanded his respect, and therefore must command theirs.

The women seemed young or middle-aged, most of them older than they looked because they had time and money to spend fighting the years. They were dressed in the height of luxurious fashion, not merely to look good but to make a statement. Not a fashion statement. Something else.

Beware!

That was it.

There was a frisson in the air, a sense of danger, and suddenly she could hear Olympia's voice saying, 'Marco's known as a lady-killer, with the emphasis on killer.'

They were watching her with hungry, glittering eyes. Curiosity, jealousy, cynicism? All these and more. Lust, envy, memories, anticipation. Some of these bold-eyed creatures had been his lovers, and wanted her to know that. And they were frankly calculating how long she could keep him faithful. Not long, some of them were doubtless thinking. They wanted her to know that, too.

She was in the lion's den.

A spurt of anger inspired her to raise her head and straighten her shoulders.

No matter that this engagement might soon be over. Tonight, at least, he was officially hers, and she would defend her right to him.

'Are you all right?' Marco asked, glancing at her.

'Fine. Never better,' she assured him.

'I believe you. This is a jungle, but you're strong.'

'I'm not scared, but perhaps they should be.'

'Yes,' he said, giving her one of his rare, brilliant smiles. 'Come,' he led her onto the floor as the music started. 'Let's tell them what they want to know.'

And they told those hot-eyed, resentful women exactly what they wanted to know, dancing close, head to head, body to body, hips moving together, seemingly lost in each other.

It was false, Harriet thought; all put on for the crowd. But the pleasure that came from just being near him was there again, infusing her limbs as they moved against his. The low-cut dress was revealing, but instead of being embarrassed, as last time, now she felt pride. She had come to believe that she was worth looking at, and she wanted this man to think so, too.

He did, if the look in his eyes was anything to go by. He seemed transfixed by her creamy bosom, her long neck, her bold eyes.

'You're beautiful,' he said softly. 'I don't want you to dance with anyone else.'

'Then I won't,' she said, smiling.

'Unfortunately you must, and so must I.'

'Yes, or all those women are going to be so disappointed.'

'Forget them.'

She laughed, so close to his face that her breath warmed him, and she felt him tremble. 'They don't want to be forgotten.'

'Forget them,' he said again. 'That's an order.'

'You give orders very easily, but it's unwise of you to tell me what to think.'

His eyes narrowed. 'Why is it "unwise"?'

'Because you should never give an order you can't enforce. How will you ever know if I'm doing what you want?'

His brow lightened. 'I shall just take it for granted that you're not. Then I can't go wrong.'

'You understand me almost as well as I understand you,' she teased.

'And what am I?'

'A tyrant.'

'And you're a witch.'

The music was coming to an end. He had just time to give her a wry look before they passed on to other partners.

The dances slid by, Count Calvani, Guido, Leo, then the local dignitaries, until finally she came to Baron Orazio Manelli.

She'd met him briefly at the start of the evening. He was younger than she had expected, middle-aged rather than elderly, strongly built with a fleshy face and a haughty expression. She'd written to him so often that she wondered if he would react to her name. He gave her an appraising look but it was hard to be sure what it meant.

Now he approached her and asked her to dance, with a look in his eye that told her he'd remembered.

'I wondered why your name was familiar,' he said genially as they took the floor. 'You've been writing to me.'

'For two years now. Everyone knows your art and sculpture collection is fabulous but you hide it away.'

'My father and my grandfather were collectors. Me, I like to spend my time among the living, not the dead. Why should a beautiful young woman like you want to bury herself in the past?'

'I love it. It's my life.'

'Not your whole life surely? Your husband will want your attention.'

'And he'll have it,' she said demurely. 'Within reason.'

He laughed so loud that heads turned. 'Marco won't let you get away with that.'

'Who says I'll ask him? I shan't stop being an antiquarian just because I'm a wife.'

He gave a throaty laugh. 'I'm beginning to like you. Perhaps we should talk some more.'

'About your collection? And me coming to see it?'

'How can I refuse you?' Somebody jostled him from behind. 'Can we go to a place that's less crowded?'

It couldn't do any harm to slip away just for a moment, she reasoned. They would go into the next room, where the party was also taking place, but where there were fewer people. But next door somebody was singing a song, so they went on further, until they reached the garden and found a bench under a tree from which hung coloured lights.

Manelli began to talk of gold, vases, jewellery, spreading a carpet of wonders before her so that her inward eyes were dazzled. The outside world slipped away. Harriet forgot where she was and what she should be doing. Time passed unnoticed as new worlds opened before her.

'But you shouldn't hide all this away,' she said fervently at last. 'With treasures like yours you should let the whole world in to see them.'

He took her hand between his two. 'One day soon you must come to my house, and it will be my pleasure to show you everything.'

'That would be wonderful,' she breathed, closing her eyes in a happy dream.

But the dream was shattered by a cold voice. 'You are neglecting our guests *cara*.'

It was Marco, standing before them, his mouth stretched in a smile that didn't reach his eyes. His gaze was fixed on her hand, tenderly enfolded between those of the Baron.

'Forgive us,' Orazio said smoothly, rising but not releasing her. 'In my wonder at discovering a lady so full of wisdom and learning, as well as so beautiful, I forgot my manners and monopolised her. May I say, Marco, how profoundly fortunate you are to have secured the affections of this delightful—'

Harriet's lips twitched. It was an outrageous performance, but an amusing one. Then she stole another look at Marco's face. He didn't find any of this funny.

'You have already conveyed your congratulations, for which I thank you,' Marco said in a wintry voice.

His stony gaze was fixed on Harriet's hand, which she quickly disentangled from Orazio, who managed to kiss it before letting go.

'I live in anticipation of your visit,' he said, 'and the time we will spend together.'

Marco's lips tightened. Harriet wanted to say, 'Don't let him tease a rise out of you. Can't you see he's doing it on purpose?' Instead she slipped her hand in the crook of his arm and walked back to the house with him.

'Don't be angry,' she said in a coaxing voice.

'Not angry?' he demanded harshly. 'Do you realise that it's nearly midnight?'

'Oh, goodness, I'm sorry. I shouldn't have been gone so long.'

'Perhaps we can discuss that later,' he said in a tight voice.

It astonished her to realise that he was taking this seriously. He knew she cared only for the treasures in Orazio's home. He was sophisticated. He should have been able to shrug it aside. But his cold fury left no doubt that this had flicked him on the raw.

They had begun to climb the steps that led up to the broad terrace that ran along the side of the house.

'Marco—'

'Let's not talk about it now. Our guests must see us in perfect accord.'

'Not if you're glowering at me.'

'I'm not. This is much simpler.'

The party had spilled out into the garden, from where the guests had a grandstand view of the terrace, and of Marco suddenly sweeping his bride into his arms and covering her face with kisses.

'I don't think—' she managed.

'Shut up,' he said savagely. 'Shut up and make it look good.'

Cheers rose from the garden as he tightened his arms in a rough simulation of desire and Harriet gave herself up to his embrace. She wouldn't have chosen it like this but she had a guilty feeling that she'd treated him badly and should help him save face.

If only he wouldn't hold her so tightly, kissing her again and again with a fierceness that looked like passion to the watchers, but which only she could sense was anger.

'Marco, don't—' she murmured. 'Enough.'

'Yes,' he said in a voice that shook. 'That's enough to convince them for the moment. Now we play the loving couple until the end of the evening.'

He loosened his grip and she swayed for a moment. Her head was spinning and she had to cling onto him. The guests, who'd crowded up onto the terrace, surrounded them, laughing and cheering at what they thought had happened. Some of the younger ones, their tongues loosened by wine, said what the rest were thinking.

'Marco, you've made the poor girl faint—'

'That's the way to kiss the woman you love—so that she really knows—'

'Now he wants to get rid of us quickly—' Roars of laughter.

'That's enough of that,' Lucia said, quelling the riot.

'We were just congratulating him,' one lad said, irrepressibly. 'Now, if Harriet were mine—'

'But she isn't,' Marco checked him. 'She's mine, and you'd be wise to remember it.' His voice was light, almost friendly. Only a few of his listeners heard the undertow of steel, and one of them was the woman standing in the circle of his arms, who could still feel that he was trembling, as she was herself. As he spoke his arm instinctively tightened about her, and she knew the message was as much for herself as for them. It was a warning.

'Bring some more champagne,' Marco called. 'Champagne for everyone.'

Servants hurried forward bearing foaming bottles, passing among the crowd until every glass was filled. Marco raised his hand for silence.

'I am the luckiest man on earth,' he said. 'The most wonderful woman in the world has promised to be my wife. There can be no greater happiness than this.'

How could he say that? she thought, when he'd all but accused her of playing him false.

How could she ever know what this man was truly thinking?

'Raise your glasses, with me, to my bride!'

They all toasted her. Over the rim of Marco's glass she saw his eyes, but couldn't discern anything behind their smile.

Then the guests toasted the two of them and the evening ended in a riot of good fellowship. It took another hour for the long, shiny cars to come, one by one, to the front door, and carry the guests away, with the family standing on the steps to bid them farewell.

When the last car had gone Harriet closed her eyes, worn out but exhilarated. Now she must make things right between herself and Marco. But when she opened her eyes again there was no sign of him.

'Don't worry,' Lucia said, seeing her look around. 'He's probably taken his cousins to his study for a whisky. Don't wait up for him.'

Harriet agreed. It might be better to let his anger cool first. She kissed Lucia goodnight and went up to her room.

She meant to shower and go to bed, but she couldn't. Something about tonight hadn't ended yet. She reached behind her neck, trying to undo the clasp of the heavy gold necklace, while one level of her mind recited the usual commentary:

French seventeenth century, genuine in gold, wrought in the style of—*oh, who cares?*

Who cared about anything except the look she'd seen in Marco's eyes when he'd found her with the Baron? What did anything matter except what that look had meant?

And then she saw it again. She hadn't heard him come into the room and the first she knew, he was there behind her, brushing her fingers aside so that he could undo the clasp. His face was so dark that she almost expected him to snatch the jewellery from her, but he removed the necklace quietly, although his fingers weren't quite steady.

'You're not still angry,' she coaxed. 'It was such a wonderful evening.'

'I'm glad you enjoyed it,' he said, tight-lipped. 'And yes, I'm still angry. You made a fool of me.'

'Just because I got into conversation with—'

'You disappeared from our engagement party with another man, and stayed away for nearly an hour,' he grated. 'Is that reason enough for you?'

'Was it really that long? I lost track of the time and forgot about—'

It was the wrong thing to say. *'You forgot!'* he snapped. 'Thank you, that was all I needed.'

'I'm sorry.'

Rage turned his voice to pure steel. 'I appreciate that your ideas of behaviour are unconventional, but did nobody ever explain to you that a woman is supposed to prefer her fiancé's company to that of any other man? If she can't manage that she's supposed to pretend. It's polite. It's the accepted thing. It stops him looking a complete fool in front of the whole world. Do you understand *that?*'

'Of course I do. Oh, look, I'm sorry Marco, I really am. I didn't mean to insult you, I just got carried away—' she saw his face. 'I'm making it worse, aren't I?'

'What you're doing is proving how English you are,' he said bitingly. 'You think having an Italian name makes you one of us, but I tell you that the name is nothing. What matters is the Italian heart and you have no idea of that.'

Harriet stared, astounded that the cool, composed man she thought she knew could have said something so cruel. 'How dare you say I'm not one of you!' she flashed. 'It's my heritage as much as yours.'

'Yes, you were born with warm Mediterranean blood in you, but it no longer speaks. Otherwise you'd know by instinct that it's vital to a man how his woman treats him.'

'I am not your woman.'

'You are—' he checked himself, then went

on. 'You are as far as people here are concerned. They think of us as a couple, but you think that means being "jolly good friends" as though a man and a woman were a pair of neuters. And only the English think like that.'

His face was like that of a stranger, watching her. 'What is it? Can't you bear the truth?'

'It isn't the truth,' she cried.

'It is the truth and you know it. You take refuge in a dead world because the living are too much for you. Your heart is fixed on the past where nothing matters and nothing can hurt. What do you know of pride, or love or passion? They're just words to you.'

'It was just carelessness,' she cried. 'It had nothing to do with love or passion—'

'But everything to do with pride,' he said bitingly. 'My pride, that you humiliated in front of everyone. What were you talking about all that time?'

'What do I ever talk about? Antiques. And you knew I was going to make a beeline for him, because I told you. You even said you'd help me get past his front door.'

'You can forget that. You're not setting foot in that man's house.'

'Are you giving me more orders?'

'Let's say I'm pointing out certain realities. He makes trouble between us. Knowing that, it's inconceivable that you should seek his company.'

'It's not his company I want. It's his art treasures.'

'You won't understand, will you? Then let me put it plainly. I forbid you to go to his house.'

'You *forbid*—? You lay down the law from on high and I'm supposed to say, "Yes sir, no sir." Boy, did you pick the wrong person! All right, I was away too long, and I'm sorry. It was inconsiderate of me. But everyone there tonight knows that this engagement was arranged. We've put on a good pretence, but there are no secrets in Rome, you told me that yourself. And if you're going to talk about pride, what about mine? There was hardly a woman there tonight who didn't—how can I put this delicately?— know you better than I do.'

'Are you saying that was a kind of revenge?' Marco asked, his eyes kindling dangerously.

'No, of course not. But nobody thinks we really mean anything to each other—'

'Mean anything to each other?' he mocked. 'What trouble you have with the word "love".'

'Love has nothing to do with this,' she said angrily. 'You can't just change the terms when it suits you.'

'The terms always included making things

look convincing, and you broke them tonight. I want your promise that you won't see him again whether I'm there or not.'

'I'll see him if I want to,' she cried. 'And the only promise I'll make is that there'll be no promises.'

'I'm warning you—'

'Don't warn me. I'm not impressed.'

'You won't see him again, Harriet, I mean it.'

'Or else what?'

'You'll find yourself on the first plane back to England.'

'In your dreams. You may be able to throw me out of this house, but would you like to bet against my moving into an hotel and visiting Manelli every day?'

His eyes narrowed. 'Don't do that. It would be an unwise move, I promise you.'

'Threats now!'

'It's not a threat, it's a promise. Do I make myself clear.'

'Perfectly, and now let me make myself clear.' She pulled off the ring and held it out to him. 'Is that clear enough?'

'Be damned to you!' With a swift movement he snatched the ring from her and hurled it away, not looking to see where it fell.

Stunned, she stared at him, realising how close he was to losing all control.

'Marco, I want you to leave now.'

She turned away but his hands were on her shoulders, forcing her back to face him. *'I haven't finished.'* She tried to wrench herself free but he kept his hands in place until she gave up.

'Let me go this minute,' she said.

'Perhaps you should take some of your own advice. Don't give an order you can't enforce. Unless you think you're strong enough to fight me.'

She didn't answer, just glared up at him from glittering, fury-filled eyes. Her struggles had caused some of her hair to fall and her cheeks were flushed. He looked her over slowly, and her wild appearance seemed to strike him, for he drew in a breath and began to pull her towards him, moving as in a trance.

'Don't you dare,' she breathed. 'Our engagement is over.'

'No,' he said, lowering his mouth. 'It isn't.'

She tried to resist but he slipped his hands down her arms, imprisoning them, giving her no choice but to accept his kiss. She'd teased him about insisting on his own way, but he was insisting now, and it was no laughing matter. This was dangerous because he had the power, which no other man had possessed, to excite her body until it turned against her, sapping her will, making her anger irrelevant.

He kissed her like a man whose knowledge of her was already so intimate that he could do as he liked. The devil himself might have kissed like that, his tongue driving into her mouth without warning, shocking, thrilling.

He knew how to use his tongue to tease and excite her, flickering it skilfully against the tender inside of her mouth, sending shivers of delight through her, then slowing, leashing himself back and her too, to her frustration.

'How dare you!' she said in a shaking voice. She was furiously angry with him for forcing this on her, and even angrier that he had stopped when her pleasure was building.

He didn't reply. She wasn't sure he'd even heard her. His face was dark, troubled, his eyes fixed on her as though asking some question that she didn't understand. One hand moved slowly up her arm to her shoulder, her neck, the fingers entwining into her hair before he dropped his head to renew the assault.

Now her arms were free, and she could push him away, except that she lacked the will. His mouth drifted over her face, bestowing teasing kisses everywhere until he reached the tender place just beneath her ear, almost as though he knew that she was unbearably sensitive just there. She took a shuddering breath at the sweet, whispering sensation that trailed down her neck to her throat, then further to the swell of her breasts.

There was no chance to pretend now. He would sense the mad beating of her heart beneath his lips. He'd challenged her to fight him but she couldn't fight the need of her own flesh that made her raise her hands, not to fend him off, but to clasp them about his head, drawing it closer. She was afire, craving more sensations that she'd never felt before with such totality. For perhaps the first time in her life she was living brilliantly, urgently in the present, and it was electrifying. A moan broke from her and she arched against him.

She felt him stiffen and become totally still. He raised his head, shaking it a little, as though wondering what was happening, then fixed his gaze on her face. She almost cried out at his expression. There was no triumph, as she'd expected, only a kind of torment.

'Marco—'

'If I ever catch you doing this with any other man,' he said hoarsely, 'I'll—I'll—'

She waited for him to finish, hearing his urgent, rasping breath and the thunder of her own heart. This was a new and bewildering Marco, tortured by some violent emotion that was close to destroying him.

'You'll do what?' she whispered at last.

A shudder went through him. 'No matter.' His grip slackened and the blazing look went out of his eyes, leaving them strangely dead.

She clung to the furniture, feeling the world still rocking beneath her. 'Perhaps it does matter,' she suggested.

'It does *not*,' he said harshly, 'because this is now closed. I apologise for alarming you.'

'Marco—'

'You have my word that it won't happen again.'

'*Marco!*'

She was looking at a closed door.

CHAPTER SEVEN

In the early morning light Harriet awoke suddenly and sat up, listening to the silence. Slipping out of bed she went to the tall window and pushed it open, looking out onto the quiet countryside, dotted with pine trees.

The memory of last night still seemed to live in every part of her, mind, heart and body. She'd seen a side of Marco she'd never dreamed of. She'd known that he was full of contradictory qualities, that he could be charming, seductive, calculating and ruthlessly determined. But she hadn't known that he could be dangerous. She knew now. For the few moments that he'd held her in his arms, forcing bruising, desperate kisses onto her, the air had crackled with danger, and she had felt alive as never before. It was shocking, but it was true.

She tried to call common sense to her aid. Whatever tumult of feeling she'd thought she detected, the truth was that Marco had been trying to prove a point. She'd made a fool of him and he wouldn't stand for it. He'd reclaimed her in front of their guests, but pride had driven him to give her a demonstration of power when they were alone. He'd wanted to show her that he could fire her with such passion that she was his, whether she liked it or not.

And he'd succeeded. She knew now what his touch could do to her. The lightest caress could melt her so that she could think only of more caresses, and more...

But his own thoughts were different, she guessed, summoning his face to her mind and trying to read his eyes. He wanted to show her that, while he wouldn't allow himself to become hers, she had no choice but to be his. In the cold light of day there was no more to it than that.

But the light of day wasn't cold. As she raised her eyes to Rome's distant hills she could see the golden glow of the rising sun.

It was nearly six in the morning. Marco, the early-rising banker, would be up by now and she needed to hear his voice. But his phone was switched off and when she called his apartment she was answered by a machine. She didn't leave a message. How could she when she didn't know what she wanted to say?

She needed to be outdoors. Hastily throwing on jeans and a sweater she slipped down the stairs and into the grounds. For a while the trees pressed close together and she was able to get away from the house, moving down winding paths that led in several directions.

That was her life now, moving along winding paths to a destination she no longer knew. A voice inside warned her to go home, but there was a bittersweet ache in her heart that said stay. She was a mass of confused feelings, and she couldn't have said where she wanted her path to lead.

She came to a small lake and began to stroll along the edge of the water, relishing the beauty of the day. The morning mist had vanished, the light was fresh, and the sound of birdsong rose in the clear air.

Where was he?

Then she saw something that made her stop and catch her breath. A man was sitting on the ground against a tree, one arm flung across his bent knee, still in the clothes he'd worn last night, but for his jacket which had been tossed aside. His shirt was open halfway down, and the way his head was flung back against the tree showed the strong, brown column of his neck, and the thick curly hair that covered his chest.

Dropping down quietly beside him Harriet saw that his eyes were closed and he breathed heavily as though sleeping. For once all tension was drained away from his features, the mouth softened, gentle, as though it had never said a harsh or bitter word. She knelt there awhile, watching his unshaven face, the hair falling over his forehead and the dark shadows beneath his eyes, feeling a tenderness he'd never inspired in her before. She knew he would hate the idea of being studied like this, while he was vulnerable and unaware, but she lingered one more moment—just one more—

He opened his eyes.

Instead of being angry he surprised her again, simply sitting motionless, gazing at her so long that she wondered if he actually saw her. At last the dazed look faded from his eyes, replaced by a helpless pain.

'You still speaking to me?' he said at last.

She nodded. There was a lump in her throat.

He sighed and dropped his head onto the arm across his knee. 'That's more than I deserve,' he said in a muffled voice. He raised his head. 'I guess I had too much to drink.'

'I didn't see you drinking very much.'

'You weren't there to see—' he checked himself with a shrug. 'Forget it.'

'Have you been out here all night?'

'Since I left you, yes.'

'I thought you were going home.'

'I had to get away from you, but I couldn't leave you, if that makes any sense.'

It made perfect sense. Since he'd stormed out last night she'd felt a persistent tug in her heart, as though it was connected to his by an invisible thread. Now she knew that he had felt it, too.

She sat down properly beside him, took one of his cold hands and began to rub it. He let her, seemingly too drained to react, but his eyes were on her hand, minus the ring.

'I haven't looked for it yet,' she explained. 'It could be anywhere in that big room. Suppose we never find it?'

His answer was the faintest possible shrug. After a moment his fingers moved to grasp hers. 'Are you all right?' he asked quietly.

'Yes, I'm fine.'

'Did I—hurt you?'

It was there again; the force of his mouth against hers, bruising, crushing, driving her wild with its ruthless persistence: the feelings still lived in her flesh, excitement, alarm, the joy of risk-taking, never known before.

'No, you didn't hurt me,' she said.

'Are you sure? I have a hellish temper, I'm afraid.'

'You weren't trying to hurt me.'

'No,' he said huskily. 'No, I was trying to make you aware of me.' His mouth quirked faintly at the corner. 'When I was a child I used to cope with frustration by roaring at the top of my voice. Then people listened.'

'Yes, I think I would have guessed something like that,' she said gently.

'Time I grew out of it, huh?'

'People don't stop being the way they are. You don't frighten me.'

'Thank God! Because that's the last thing I'd ever want. Please Harriet, forget everything about last night.'

'Everything? You mean—?'

'Every last damned thing,' he said emphatically. 'Go to Manelli's house whenever you like. There'll be no more trouble, I promise. What's past is past. It was a kind of madness, no more.'

'But Marco, what got into you? It wasn't drink, I know that.'

'I can't explain, but there are some things I'm not—rational about. Let's just say that I get jealous easily. And possessive. It's not nice. I apologise.'

'You have nothing to be jealous about.'

'I know. But there are things I can't forget.'

'About the other woman, the one you were going to marry?'

He stirred. 'What do you know about her?'

'Not much. You were engaged, then you both changed your mind.'

A long silence, then he said as though the words were dredged up from some fearful depths. 'It was a little more complicated than that.'

'Break ups aren't usually completely equal,' she suggested tentatively.

He nodded. 'Something of the kind. Whatever! It makes me act unreasonably, and I'm sorry.'

She gave his hand a reassuring squeeze, thinking that she'd never in her life seen a man so unhappy.

'When you find the ring,' he said wearily, 'will you wear it again?'

She hesitated. 'I don't know.'

'If you leave now—so soon after last night—' he gave a bark of laughter. 'That'll give the gossips something to talk about. And also—' he grew quiet again '—it would hurt my mother badly.'

'I won't leave—for the moment.'

'Thank you.'

Suddenly he leaned forward, resting his head against her in an attitude of despondency, almost of despair, she thought. Her arms went about him and she held him close, longing to comfort him, but knowing that there was a part of him she still couldn't reach. She dropped her own head, resting her cheek against his dishevelled hair, and tried to tell him, through the strength of her embrace, that she was there for him. She thought she felt his arms tighten about her, as though he'd found something he needed to cling to.

They sat motionless while the warmth stole through her. Not the warmth of passion: something quite different and far more alarming. While they fought she could hold out against him, even in the face of her own desire. But his sudden vulnerability shook desire into a fierce longing to protect him that was suspiciously like love.

Disaster! She hadn't meant to love him, wasn't sure she wanted to. It was a trap and she'd fallen into it before she knew it was there.

Why couldn't you have gone on driving me nuts? she thought. It was easier then. This isn't fair.

He stirred and she released him. He pushed back his hair, which immediately fell over his forehead again. 'I suppose I look like a tramp?'

'A bit,' she said tenderly.

He started to get up and winced. 'I'm stiff!'

'If you've been here all night I'm not surprised. Let me help.'

He slipped an arm about her neck and got painfully to his feet, scooping up his leaf-stained jacket.

'The ground's damp,' she said. 'You could catch pneumonia like this.'

'I used to sleep out a lot when I was a kid. Just over there in the woods, there's a place where I'd make a camp and pretend I was an outlaw.'

'Show me.' She wanted to prolong this gentle time with him.

'All right.'

Still with his arm around her shoulders he guided her through the trees and up a steep slope to a clearing. 'This is where I used to sleep out under the stars,' he said.

'It's a wonderful view.'

'Yes, "the enemy" couldn't approach you unaware.'

'Unless they came from above,' she pointed out. 'But I expect you posted sentries. How many of you were there?'

'Just me. I used to envy Leo and Guido who were brothers and had each other. Actually they were separated when Guido was ten, and Uncle Francesco took him to live in Venice, leaving Leo in Tuscany. But I always thought of them as having each other.'

'It's a pity you didn't have any brothers and sisters.'

'My father died early, and Mamma never wanted to marry again.'

'But surely you had some friends?'

He shrugged. 'At school.'

But none for his fantasy life, she thought, pitying the lonely little boy. She thought of how much easier he was when surrounded by the rest of the boisterous Calvani family, like a man who would gladly be one of them, but always felt slightly apart.

'You can see almost as far as Rome from this spot,' he said. 'At night I used to sit under this tree and watch the lights. Just here.' He put his jacket on the ground and indicated for her to sit on it beside him.

'You too,' she said, making room for him.

They sat quietly together as the light expanded and the sound of birdsong grew louder. His hand had found its way into hers.

'This is a wonderful place,' she said. 'I can understand you wanting to come here often.'

There was no answer, and she became aware of a weight on her shoulder. Turning, she found his head lying against her, his eyes closed again.

Now she saw something else in his face. He was weary in a way that had nothing to do with missed sleep. Strain and tension had fallen away, but they left behind a bone-deep exhaustion that looked as if it had been there a long time, perhaps years.

She'd never thought to pity Marco, but she

pitied him now in a way that she didn't entirely understand. But there would be time to learn about him, and reach out to the trouble deep within him. Gently she brushed the hair back from his forehead.

He stirred and opened his eyes, looking straight into her smiling ones.

'You fell asleep again,' she said tenderly.

'Yes—' he sounded unsure of himself. 'How long?'

'Just a few minutes.'

Then she saw the look that she'd dreaded, as though shutters had come down. Light faded from his eyes, leaving a deliberate emptiness as he withdrew back into the comfortless place within himself. He pulled away from her and got to his feet, not letting her assist him this time, but offering his own hand to help her up. She took it, rising so quickly that she almost lost her balance. He steadied her with his other hand on her arm, but didn't draw her close, as he could so easily have done.

With dismay she realised that it was all gone, the warmth and communication that had been there before. Now his eyes were watchful. Perhaps he was even more wary of her because he'd allowed her to draw near.

'What time is it?' he asked, consulting his

watch. 'Past seven. I've got to be going. I'm sorry for putting all this onto you.'

'I'm glad we talked,' she said, seeking a way back to him. 'I understand you better now.'

He shrugged. 'What is there to understand? I behaved badly, for which I'm sorry. You've been very patient, but there's no reason for you to put up with my moods. I won't inflict them on you again.'

She nearly said, 'Not even when we're married?' but the words wouldn't come. Everything that had seemed certain a moment ago had vanished into illusion. She no longer knew him.

She made one last try. 'Moods aren't the worst thing in the world. Maybe people shouldn't be polite all the time. I wasn't very polite to you last night and you—'

'Overreacted I'm afraid. But it won't happen again. Now, can we leave it?'

He rubbed his stubbled jaw. 'I'd better get inside and put myself right. I don't want my mother to see me like this. I'd prefer that you didn't tell her.'

'Of course not.'

They walked back in silence. Within sight of the house he said, 'Take a look first, and signal me if it's clear. No, wait!'

He grasped her arm and pulled her back into

the trees as Lucia appeared at the rear door. Her voice reached them.

'Who left this door unlocked? Surely it hasn't been like this all night?'

'It's all right,' Harriet said, advancing so that Lucia could see her. 'I opened it. I've been out for an early-morning walk.'

She ran up the steps, kissed Lucia and drew her inside, chattering, apparently aimlessly, but actually manoeuvring her deep into the house. She resisted the temptation to look back, but she thought she heard the faint sound of footsteps going up the stairs.

Half an hour later Marco joined them for breakfast, showered, impeccably dressed and apparently his normal self. He thanked his mother charmingly for the successful party and complimented Harriet on her successful debut in society. He made no mention of anything else.

A few days later an invitation arrived to a party at the Palazzo Manelli.

'We've never been invited there before,' Lucia observed in surprise.

'It's Harriet he really wants, Mamma,' Marco said. 'She's after his collection.' He gave Harriet a brief smile. 'This will make your name. Nobody's ever been so privileged before. Of course we must accept.'

Nobody could have faulted his manner, which was charming, but impenetrable.

Life at the villa had settled into a contented routine. Lucia, whose days were filled with committees, was happy for her guest to spend her time in museums and art galleries. They would meet in the evening for a meal sometimes at home, sometimes at a restaurant before going to the opera. On these occasions Marco would usually join them after the meal, and Harriet realised that he loved opera. Comedies didn't interest him, but he was drawn to the emotional melodramas, and would sit through the music in a kind of brooding trance, emerging reluctantly.

She'd found the ring and slipped it back onto her finger for public occasions, explaining to Lucia that at other times she was afraid of losing it. She wore it when Marco invited her to lunch again at the bank. He was delightful, even amusing, but she felt he was sending her a silent message that there was no way back to the brief closeness they'd known.

'You're afraid I'll make trouble at Manelli's party, but I've already promised not to,' he said smoothly. 'And nobody will think anything of it if such a noted antiquarian as yourself goes off to explore. No, don't look so sceptical. I'm learning about your international reputation. Several of my colleagues here recognised your name and have asked to meet you.' He raised his glass. 'I'm very proud of my fiancée.'

Of his fiancée, she noted, not of herself. There was no way past such implacable charm.

The Palazzo Manelli was in the heart of Rome's old quarter, near St Peter's. The lights were already blazing forth from wide windows and doors as their car glided up. The Baron was there to greet them.

Harriet enjoyed herself from the first moment. She knew she was looking at her best in a dress of deep gold silk, with Marco's gift of rubies about her neck, and she was already acquainted with many of the people here.

Marco squired her conscientiously at first, introducing her to the few strangers, making clear his pride and admiration. Then, true to his promise, he faded away and turned his attention to other guests. These were his old friends and could keep him happily occupied all evening. All his fiancée required was the occasional glance to see if she needed his help. Which she never did.

As Harriet's confidence grew her wit flowered. Manelli's guests included several nationalities, and her ability to riposte quickly in each of their languages was making heads turn. This, plus her physical transformation, had made her into a 'figure', a slightly exotic personality. She wasn't pretty, but she was magnificent, and every man in the place seemed increasingly aware of it.

'Marco, what are you doing neglecting poor Harriet?' Lucia chided him.

'"Poor" Harriet is doing very well without me.' Marco said calmly. 'Does she look neglected?'

'She looks submerged in men,' Lucia retorted tartly. 'One of them is positively drooling over her hand, and the other keeps trying to see down her dress.'

'Mamma, the man trying to see down her dress owns an original Michelangelo piece of sculpture,' Marco said, as if that explained everything. 'I can't compete with that. And it's all perfectly innocent.'

'Hmph! Manelli isn't innocent. He's one of the worst lechers in Rome.'

'But Harriet is innocent, which is what counts.' Then he drew a sharp breath.

'What is it? My dear boy, why do you look like that?'

'Nothing,' he said, pulling himself together. 'Please don't trouble yourself about this,

Mamma. It's the modern way. Engaged couples don't live in each other's pockets. Will you excuse me for a moment?'

He moved away quickly, feeling that if he couldn't be alone soon he would suffocate. In the garden he managed to evade the lights and laughter and find solitude under the dark trees. His forehead was damp with the strain of what had just happened to him.

He'd said, 'Harriet is innocent,' and the word 'innocent' had been like a bullet, shattering the glass wall he kept between himself and the past. *She's innocent—innocent.* That was what he'd said when they had tried to warn him about the woman to whom he'd given his heart once and for all time, with nothing held back. No defences. No suspicions, even when he heard the rumours. Just blind love. Blind and stupid. A mistake, never to be repeated. For she hadn't been innocent, and he'd found out in a way so brutal that it had almost destroyed him. Memory returned to him now, leaving him shaking like a man in the grip of fever.

But Harriet was different, not merely innocent but guileless and blinkered, as only the truly honest were. And there lay his safety, he reasoned. In the long run it was more reliable than trusting to her, or any woman's, heart.

After a while he pulled himself together.

When he was sure he could appear his normal self he returned to the party, smiling broadly, not letting his eyes search for her.

Harriet was relishing her success. After squiring her around at first Marco had turned away with a smile, leaving her to her own devices, and thereafter he entertained himself with all the most beautiful women. Which suited her fine, she thought. Just fine.

And then she saw someone who drove all other thoughts out of her mind.

'Olympia!'

Her sister had just arrived, now she came sweeping across the floor, arms open to envelope Harriet, pretty face full of glee.

'I've been hearing so much about you,' she cried, managing to whisper under cover of their embrace. 'Are you really engaged to Marco?'

'I'm not sure,' Harriet said wryly.

Olympia stood back and regarded her. 'There's my cautious Harriet. If only I could learn from you!'

'Then you wouldn't be Olympia,' Harriet laughed. 'Where have you been all this time?'

'In America, with Mamma and Poppa. They're still there, but I came home today, and rushed here because I heard ''Marco and his bride'' were going to be at the party. Oh, you clever, clever sister. You got your own terms, then?'

'Well—'

'But of course you did. My dear, *that ring!* It must have cost—'

'Don't be vulgar,' Harriet chuckled.

'You're right. Play it cool. Keep him guessing. That's the way with Marco. And the others as well. They say you've got Manelli eating out of your hand.'

'He's going to show me around.'

Manelli appeared at that very moment and swept both women off for a tour of his mansion. He talked well and informatively, and Olympia's eyes were soon glazing with boredom. She made a desperate excuse and escaped, barely noticed by either of them.

Returning to the party, she was immediately claimed by admirers, and worked her way through them until she found Marco. He hadn't seen her since the day he'd made his proposition and she'd rejected him in five seconds. They greeted each other amiably.

'I didn't know what I was starting when I suggested Harriet, did I?' she teased. 'Did I do you a bad turn?'

'Not at all. Harriet is an excellent choice, barring her habit of vanishing with other men at parties.'

'Oh, Manelli's just showing her his pictures. No need to be jealous.'

'Don't be ridiculous. Of course I'm not jealous.'

'All right, don't snap at me. Harriet's a very unexpected person, as I dare say you know by now. I must admit I only suggested her to tease a rise out of you.'

'The sort of prank I'd have expected from you,' he said coldly. 'You haven't grown up since you were a child and I used to rescue you from trees when you'd climbed too far. I can take care of myself, but did you ever think you were being unfair to Harriet?'

'You mean she might have fallen for you?' Olympia asked with a trill of laughter. 'Nonsense, *caro*. I wouldn't have done it if I thought she might get hurt. I know you're incapable of falling in love, but so is she. Haven't you found that out yet?'

She passed on, saving him the necessity of replying.

CHAPTER EIGHT

MARCO had said Harriet had an international reputation and she was discovering how true it was. The news that she had broken 'the Manelli barrier' was soon all over Rome, and her services began to be much in demand.

'I'm here as an emissary,' Marco said to her one evening. 'Two of my colleagues at work want to consult you and they say you're putting them off. I've promised to use my influence. They seem to think I have some,' he added drily.

'I was being tactful,' Harriet said. 'Precisely because they're your colleagues it seemed better for me to stay clear. Suppose I give them wrong advice?'

'Is that possible?' he murmured slyly.

'Tell them about the necklace,' she challenged him.

'The less said about that necklace the better,' he said, almost teasing. 'May I inform my associates that my influence has been successful?'

'I'll bet you've already done so.'

He grinned and didn't deny it.

On this level they were easy with each other, but Harriet had learned that any attempt to draw closer to him was fruitless. After that one time in the garden he'd retreated into his shell, perhaps further back than before, wary, mistrustful of her and himself. Above all, mistrustful of what might happen between them.

It was lucky that she hadn't fallen in love with him, as she'd briefly feared. The moment when she'd sensed approaching disaster had been a warning which 'sensible Harriet', now in the ascendant again, had heeded. Soon the time would come for them to go their separate ways, him to find a suitable bride elsewhere, and herself into an apartment in the city.

For she'd decided to stay here. With Marco's help she'd reclaimed her Italian heritage, and she would always be grateful to him for that. But as more people sought her expertise she realised that she was laying the groundwork for a life here that didn't include him.

So when he asked her to accompany him on a trip to visit a client, who lived in Corzena, about two hundred miles to the north of Rome, she had no trouble in claiming that her time was occupied.

'You can surely spare a couple of days for me,' he said impatiently.

'I'm busy.'

'Doing what?'

'I beg your pardon!'

'It can't be that important.'

'That's for me to say,' she insisted, riled by his tone. *'Give me that!'*

He'd snatched up the pad on which she'd scribbled notes on her current work.

'The Vatican Museum,' he read.

'Signor Carelli has asked me to check some references for him.' This should have been the killer fact, since Carelli was one of the banking colleagues for whom Marco had interceded. But he wasn't impressed.

'He won't mind waiting,' he said.

She knew it was true. She was finding excuses, and she wasn't sure exactly why, except that she felt herself subtly moving away from him, and perhaps it was best to keep it that way.

'I'm not going to ask him to wait,' she said firmly. 'I've made my plans and I'd prefer to stick to them.'

'Fine,' he said, tight-lipped. 'I won't ask again. Please tell my mother I called, and that I'll be away for the rest of the week.'

And when he'd gone it all seemed so stupid. Why had she taken such a stubborn line? Why refuse to spend a couple of days in his company?

Because the prospect was far too agreeable, that was the answer. It was a relief that he'd left, making it too late to change her mind. Not that she wanted to change her mind.

Lucia slept late next day and Harriet breakfasted alone. She was just finishing her coffee when Marco walked in. Her heart's flicker of delight was too intense to be ignored, but she concealed it.

'I thought you'd be on your way by now,' she exclaimed. 'Weren't you leaving early?'

He'd left in the dawn and driven for twenty miles before stopping the car and getting out to stand looking over the countryside. He'd stayed there for half an hour before getting back into the car and turning it around.

'I've come back because I want you to be honest with me,' he said quietly. 'I want the real reason you won't come to Corzena.'

'I've already told you—'

'Yes, you have, and it's bull. You know it and I know it. I want the other reason—' he faced her '—the one you can't bring yourself to tell me.'

Alarm and pleasure seized her equally. Had he really guessed that she'd turned coward, backing off because she feared the growing strength of her own feelings for a man who was incapable of returning them? Or did he return them, and this was his way of creating the mood for a declaration?

'Marco—'

'Harriet,' he said desperately, 'I know. Did you really think I wouldn't guess?'

'You've guessed—?' she whispered, not daring to hope.

'When I started to think hard it became obvious—especially after what happened the night of the party— Harriet, I may not be the most sensitive man in the world, but I think I'm sensitive enough to see this. We've been honest with each other from the start, why didn't you just tell me—? No, that's stupid, isn't it? How could you speak bluntly about such a delicate matter?'

'Marco, are you saying—?'

'I'll make it easy for you by saying it myself.' He took a deep breath, evidently having difficulty, and she waited, her heart beating eagerly. At last he said, 'You don't want to be alone with me. You're afraid of what I'll do.'

'Wh-what?'

'That's it, isn't it? You don't trust me, to behave decently. But you can, I swear it.'

She was coming out of her happy daze to a chilly reality. 'I see,' she managed to say, hoping desperately that her face didn't show her cruel disappointment.

'This is business,' he went on, 'and my client is an important one. The bank tends to indulge his wishes, and his present wish is to meet you.'

'That's blackmail!'

'Yes, I suppose it is, and that's just why you can trust me. Having more or less coerced you into this trip the last thing I'd do would be put you in an awkward situation.' He regarded her steadily. 'I hope you understand me.'

She wanted to laugh, perhaps hysterically. 'I think I do. You're promising to be the perfect gentleman, no midnight taps on my door—'

'I doubt our rooms will even be on the same floor. Our host is very old-fashioned. Nothing will happen, Harriet, you have my word of honour.'

She wanted to throw something at him and scream, I don't want your word of honour. I don't want you to be the perfect gentleman. I want you to kiss me as you did that night, and this time I don't want you to stop. Oh, you idiot!

But instead she said coolly, 'I suppose, that makes everything all right.'

'I hoped it would. This is really important, he's a very big client—'

'Then we must keep him happy,' she said brightly. 'Business comes first, after all.'

He smiled at her. 'You say that to the manner born.'

'You think I might be a credit to you?'

He put his hands on her shoulders, smiling into her eyes in a way that made her hold her breath. If only—

'You already are a credit to me,' he said warmly. 'I'm proud of you and I want to show you off. Get some clothes together quickly, while I go and see if my mother's awake.'

As she packed she heard murmurs coming from Lucia's room, and went in to bid her good-bye. 'I'm sorry to rush off without notice—'

'Nonsense. Go on and have a wonderful time, *cara*.'

It was a lovely day and their drive lay through beautiful countryside. Gradually her mood improved from the sheer pleasure of being with him. Marco drove fast but easily and with confidence, as he did everything.

'Tell me about this man,' she said.

'Elvino Lucci is one of the richest men in Italy. He started with nothing and he's built up to where he is through sheer hard work and brilliance. He's been my mentor for years.'

'I can't picture you with a mentor, somehow. I don't think you'd let him get a word in edgeways.'

'Everyone needs a mentor,' he said seriously.

'Not just at the start but maybe for always, to give you a sense of perspective. I learned a lot from him when I was just starting, and he still has things to teach me.'

'A great financial brain, then?'

'The greatest. He believed in keeping his attention focused and never taking his eye off the ball.'

'You mean there's been nothing in his life but financial wheeling and dealing?'

'He married and has a family, but he's been a widower for ten years.'

'I'll bet he married an heiress.'

'No, his own secretary.'

'Oh, well, nothing like securing cheap labour.'

Marco laughed. 'You may find him a little stiff and puritanical, but you'll like him when you get to know each other.'

'But why does he want to meet me?' she asked lightly. 'Am I being tested for suitability? If he gives me the thumbs down, am I out?'

'Don't be absurd. I think he's just lonely.'

'Lonely? With all that money?'

'Harriet please don't say that kind of thing in front him? I know it's a joke, but he wouldn't understand.'

'Hey, you recognised a joke. Better not let

him suspect that, or you might not be his white-headed boy any more.'

Diplomatically he didn't answer this.

When they stopped for lunch Marco called Elvino Lucci to apologise for being late. Harriet could just make out the man's voice.

'You, late? That must be a first! Only something special would make Marco Calvani break the habits of a lifetime!'

'It was,' Marco said.

'Well, I'm longing to meet her. I'm storing up a little surprise myself.'

They reached Corzena in the late afternoon. It was an old town built on a hill at the edge of a lake, with the villa on the lower part, near the shore. Huge wrought-iron gates swung open at their approach, and soon the house was in sight. There on the steps, waiting to greet them, was a tall man with white hair and a distinguished face. Beside him stood a very young woman who bore a strong resemblance to a sugar-coated doll. She had a mass of blonde hair, dressed high and wide, and sprayed into a confection like candyfloss. Her eyes were large and ingenuous.

'Good grief!' Marco murmured. 'What—'

Lucci advanced to greet them with outstretched arms. After kissing Harriet on both cheeks, he sprang his surprise.

'Meet Ginetta, my wife,' he said. 'We married on impulse, and you're the first to know.'

Marco maintained his composure, greeting the new Signora Lucci with perfect courtesy, but Harriet could imagine his thoughts. Elvino was at least thirty years older than his bride, and clearly took pleasure in buying her jewels. She was loaded down with them.

There was another shock awaiting. Marco had described Lucci as a man of old-fashioned values, but now Ginetta gave the orders, and her idea of how to accommodate an engaged couple was modern. While not going so far as to put them in the same room she'd given them adjoining rooms with a connecting door.

'We'll be waiting downstairs when you've freshened up,' she cooed, tripping daintily away.

When she'd gone Marco knocked on Harriet's door before entering.

'I hope you realise that I had no idea of this,' he said. 'I never meant to break my word to you.'

'I know that. You're not responsible for them putting us together.'

'Whatever is Lucci thinking of?'

'He's in love with her, that's obvious.'

'To think of him springing it on me! This visit is going to be an ordeal.'

At first Harriet thought the same, but it wasn't long before she began to like Ginetta, who seemed genuinely fond of her elderly husband, if not as besotted by him as he was by her. She also had a habit of making apparently naïve remarks that turned out, on examination, to be shrewd and witty. Several times over dinner Harriet found herself laughing.

After the meal Ginetta insisted on showing her over the villa, innocently proud of its luxury and her own good fortune in securing a husband who could lavish gifts on her. Even so, her happiness had a cloud.

'I'm really glad you came,' she confided. 'I made Vinni absolutely promise to get you here. Lots of wives don't want to know me.'

'I can't think why,' Harriet said warmly. 'I think you're great fun. But I'm not Marco's wife, you know.'

'But you soon will be. He's nuts about you, anyone can see that.'

Harriet gave a little laugh that sounded odd to herself. 'It's not Marco's way to be ''nuts''. And if he was he'd die rather than admit it.'

'It's just there in the way he looks at you, when you're not looking back. He does it all the time. He can't stop himself.'

'Nonsense,' Harriet said, colouring.

'It's true. And you do it, too.'

'I—'

'Yes, you do. You two fancy each other like crazy. It's a good thing I gave you connecting rooms.'

It was fortunate that she tripped away, calling back, 'Come on, let's find the men,' because Harriet wouldn't have known how to answer.

The men were sitting on the broad terrace that overlooked the lake, drinking brandy and deep in discussion. Harriet could see that Marco was displeased, although controlling it beneath a courteous front. Both men rose to greet them. Elvino ordered more champagne and they all strolled along the terrace, watching the moonlight on the water.

This joyful man bore no relation at all to the severe, practical 'brain' Marco had described, and which he clearly admired. He was triumphant in his happiness, wanting everyone to share it, laughing and kissing Ginetta repeatedly.

'This is truly a house of love,' he declared exuberantly, 'since it houses two pairs of lovers. I drink to your coming wedding, I drink to your wedding night, I drink to all the pleasure you will take in each other—'

'*Caro,*' Ginetta giggled.

'Oh, they don't mind. They're lovers, as we are.' He was becoming jollier with every glass, and there was no stopping him now. 'Come Marco, drink with me to the woman you love.'

Harriet could hardly look at Marco, guessing how he would regard such a boisterous display. But he said quietly, 'You are right, my friend. Let us drink.'

He raised his glass in Harriet's direction, she raised hers, and they clinked.

'Don't just drink to the girl,' Elvino bawled. 'Kiss her, and then kiss her again. And let your kisses be a pledge of the passion to come.'

To demonstrate his point he tightened the arm that was about Ginetta's shoulders, and gave her a smacking kiss. Marco responded by drawing Harriet close and laying his lips on hers. For a moment she raised her hands against him. She didn't want to kiss him like this, knowing he'd been forced by politeness, and when he'd been at such pains to assure her that he would keep his distance.

His lips lay lightly on hers, but that was somehow more unnerving than the night she'd sensed his fierce desire. He took her hand, still raised in an instinctive gesture of resistance.

'Kiss me back,' he murmured against her lips. 'Make it look good.'

Make it look good for the client, she thought angrily. But her hand was already reaching up to touch his face, while the other arm wound its way around him. His own arms tightened, drawing her very close. His lips moved across hers, subtly enticing, almost the ghost of a kiss, but a ghost that was enfolding her in a mysterious spell. She let herself slip into that spell easily, for now it was all right to caress his face and press against him, putting her whole heart and soul into what she was doing. He need never know. She was merely helping him keep a client happy.

Marco too played his part with conviction, slipping an arm beneath her neck and kissing her with a kind of dreamy absorption that she thought must delude anybody. Except her. The slow movement of his lips over hers was sweet, blissful, and the temptation to believe in it was overpowering. She opened her eyes to find his face hovering close, his eyes fixed on her with a kind of astonishment. He was breathing unevenly.

From Elvino came another burst of delight. 'That's the spirit,' he bawled. 'And now there's only one thing to do—carry the lady upstairs.'

On the word he lifted Ginetta and began to walk along the terrace, calling, 'Time for lovers to go to bed,' over his shoulder.

Marco didn't hesitate, and the next moment Harriet found herself lifted against his chest.

She clung to him dizzily, confused as to how to get her bearings, but not really wanting to.

Elvino reached the top of the stairs first and stopped to wait for them.

'This is the way to live,' he said blissfully. 'Oh, I know that's not what I used to say, but I'm wiser now. So are you, eh, my boy?'

'You were always a wise man, Lucci,' Marco murmured diplomatically.

'Goodnight, goodnight—' His voice drifted away along the corridor.

But at the last minute he turned, just as Marco reached Harriet's bedroom door. The old man's eyes glinted with fun as Harriet turned the handle and Marco carried her in. She could feel him trembling, as she was herself.

Once inside he set her down and closed the door.

'You'd better lock it,' she said in a shaking voice that was half-laughter and half-excitement. 'I wouldn't put it past him to bounce in to see if we're living up to his expectations.'

'Harriet, please—let me apologise for—everything. I never meant to embarrass you like this—'

'I'm not embarrassed. I like him. Don't you?'

'I don't know any more. I used to respect

him. There wasn't a shrewder brain anywhere—now I can't think what's gotten into him.'

'No,' she said wryly. 'I don't suppose you can.'

'He's always been so sane and level-headed.'

'Well, maybe he thinks being sane and level-headed is overrated. Marco, he's happy. Don't you realise that?'

She smiled, willing him to lighten up.

'Happy!' Marco said scathingly.

'It's generally considered a good thing to be.'

He began to stride about the room. 'And what happens when she betrays him?'

'Maybe she never will. Yes, I'm sure she married for security, but I think she's got a kind heart. She's nice to him.'

'She leads him by the nose, makes him her slave—'

'No, he makes himself her slave, because he loves her.'

'That's one way of putting it.'

'You don't think much of love, do you, Marco?'

'You're unjust to me,' he said after a moment. 'I think love has its place, but I don't like the kind of infatuation that makes a man behave like an imbecile.'

'Or woman?'

'Oh, no! Women are always one jump ahead, as *Signora Lucci* more than proves.'

'That's the most disgusting prejudice I ever heard. Women do make idiots of themselves over men—'

'You never felt it necessary. It's one of the things I've always admired about you. Your level head. Even that tomfool performance we had to put on out there didn't faze you.'

'Shut up!' she breathed. 'Shut up, *shut up!*' If she had to hear any more of this she would go mad.

'I apologise if I was being rude—'

'*And stop apologising!*' She took a long breath and pulled herself together. 'We're getting off the subject. There's nothing wrong with acting like an imbecile for the right person. If people really love, they don't care about that—'

'God help them then!' he said violently. 'And God help Lucci for acting like a fool!'

'But he's a happy fool.'

Marco stopped pacing and gave her a strange look. 'That's just sentimental talk, Harriet. It sounds good but it means nothing. No fool is really happy, because sooner or later he sees his folly and is ashamed of it. Then he wishes he'd never met her.'

'You're wrong about Elvino,' Harriet said fervently. 'He'll never be sorry he met Ginetta because even if he loses his happiness he'll still have had it. If he was wise, like you think he should be, he'd end up with nothing at all.'

His face was bleak. 'Better to have nothing than shame and bitterness.'

She sighed. 'Well, how do you choose between them? The man who believes in someone he loves, even if it makes him a little absurd, or the man who won't let himself believe in anyone? Who's the real fool, I wonder?'

He gave a hard little laugh. 'You mean me, don't you? Stop trying to analyse me, Harriet, you don't know enough.'

'Then tell me the rest,' she pleaded.

'It's not important,' he said impatiently. 'I am as I am. I can't change now.'

'That's the sad part. You have just so much to give, and no more.'

He went a little pale. 'I give all I can.'

'I know. But it isn't very much, is it?'

He was silent for a long moment, turning away to the window. When he turned back he said, 'You think badly of me because I don't fall over myself to endorse Lucci's idiocy. Well, consider this. He brought me here to help him hand over half his fortune to that little gold-digger.'

'She's his wife and she's making him happy,'

Harriet said desperately. She felt as if she was banging her head against stone. Like his heart.

'He has four children who are going to lose half of their inheritance, only they don't know it yet. The lawyer's coming tomorrow, and he and I between us are supposed to connive at this disgrace. Plus I've broken a professional confidence by telling you.'

'You can trust me.'

'I never doubted that for a moment.'

It was lucky he'd turned back to the window or he might have seen the painful look that crossed her face. Her fiancé trusted her with his professional secrets. From a man with such a strong code of ethics it was high praise, but not the kind she longed for.

'It's late,' she said sadly. 'And I'm tired.'

'Then I won't keep you up any longer.' He opened the connecting door. 'Don't forget to lock this behind me,' he said with an attempt at lightness.

She matched his tone. 'Do I need to?'

'I wouldn't put it past Lucci to send an army in here to make sure I "do my duty". Goodnight, Harriet.'

She undressed and lay in the darkness, every inch of her aware and aching with longing. Elvino's romantic insistence on love at all costs had left her fired up, ready for something to happen.

Tonight she and Marco had talked of one thing while seeming to talk about another and the end of it was that she was no closer to him in any way that mattered. Just in one way.

You two fancy each other like crazy.

It was almost funny that Ginetta had spotted the strong physical attraction that she felt for him and that he, she was sure, felt for her. He couldn't love her but he wanted her. If he had his free choice now he would come to her bed.

But he had no free choice. He'd blocked it off with promises. He was a man of his word, and would resist what he saw as a weakness.

How badly did he want her?

She could hear him walking back and forth on the other side of the door.

Badly enough to break his word?

His footsteps stopped, then resumed again.

Badly enough to risk looking weak in his own eyes?

Silence. The footsteps had stopped right next to the door.

Holding her breath, Harriet kept her eyes fixed on the handle, which she could just see in the moonlight.

Very slowly it moved. There was the faintest

noise as the door was opened a fraction, perhaps half an inch. Then it stopped.

She waited for it to move again, to open. She couldn't breathe. She could almost feel the air vibrating with the tormented indecision of the man on the other side. But he would come to her because she willed it so fiercely.

But then the incredible happened. Instead of opening further the door moved back, closing the tiny gap, and the handle was softly returned into place.

After that there was silence.

CHAPTER NINE

IT WAS a relief to spend a few days in the Vatican museum. Absorbed in the world that had always sustained her, Harriet thought she would soon be able to forget Corzena.

But the talisman failed this time. Halfway through a fourteenth-century parchment she would find herself thinking of the door that had so nearly opened, and then closed.

Closed against her. That was the thing that hurt. Marco had tested the door just far enough to discover that she'd left it open for him. Then he had rejected her. What message could be clearer?

From their manner to each other on the drive home nobody could have discerned anything in the air. For him, there probably hadn't been, she thought bitterly.

She returned home on the third evening to find Lucia eagerly looking for her.

'Your father called,' she said. 'They're back, and so anxious to see you. We're all three invited to dine tomorrow night. I tried to call you and Marco but you both had your phones switched off. So I said yes for us all. Did I do right?'

'Of course. My father! How did he sound?'

'Thrilled by your engagement. He's longing to see you. I found him almost likeable. I'm sorry, *cara*, I know he's your father, but there it is. But if he's good to you, I forgive him everything.'

Marco arrived for supper and heard the whole story.

'It makes a tight schedule now we're so busy getting ready to go to Venice for the weddings,' Lucia observed. 'But when I suggested putting it off until we returned he was most insistent that it must be tomorrow. Still, it's natural that he should be eager to see you.'

'It's a tighter schedule than you know,' Marco said. 'After tonight I was planning to sleep at my office to get through everything that needs doing before we leave for Venice.'

'I suppose you could always ask your uncle and Guido to delay their weddings?' Harriet suggested in the satirical tone she often used to him.

'True,' Marco said, appearing to consider this seriously. 'But they're so unreasonable that they'd probably put their weddings before my clients.'

He smiled at her to show that he was sharing the joke. Harriet wondered if she really had been joking. This was the first time she'd seen him since Corzena, and he'd just told her that after tomorrow she wouldn't see him again for days. To her dismay she discovered that it was a relief.

To cheer herself up she concentrated on the thought of her father.

'Tell me everything he said,' she begged Lucia.

'Again? All right, *cara*, I understand. He asked after you many times, were you well, were you happy in your engagement, could he give you to Marco with an easy mind? All the questions a loving father asks.'

'And which he's waited a very long time to ask,' Marco said drily. 'I wonder what lies behind this.'

'Does my father's interest need an explanation?' Harriet flashed.

'His *sudden* interest does.'

'I'm engaged. Isn't that enough?'

'Yes, I suppose so. Now, it's late and I must be going.'

She treated herself to a new gown for the following evening, elegant, figure-hugging black silk that made a perfect setting for

Marco's gift of a diamond tiara. The hairdresser settled it into her upswept hair.

She touched the diamonds, feeling how cold they were: as cold as his attempt to spoil the evening in advance by his sceptical remarks about her father. But why should he have done so? she wondered. He could be hard, unfeeling, but this had felt like a deliberate attempt to hurt her.

She and Lucia were to travel together in the chauffeur-driven car, while Marco drove straight there from work. The d'Estinos lived in Rome's most fashionable quarter, near St Peter's, in a street where most of the other buildings were embassies. As they arrived they could see Marco getting out of his own car. He glanced at Harriet's magnificence and nodded.

'I knew that tiara was right for you,' he said. 'Not every woman could wear it.'

As they approached the wide front doors, standing open, flooding the gardens with light, her father appeared, flinging wide his arms and bearing down on her. 'Harriet, my dearest daughter. After so long.'

He embraced her in a bear hug, the first for years. He was wearing an overpowering cologne, and she had to fight not to flinch. He looked older than his years, and had put on too much weight, giving a strong impression of self-indulgence, and her acute instincts told her that there was something false and theatrical about this display.

But he was her father and she'd longed for this moment, so she smiled and told herself how wonderful it was.

He was all smiles to Lucia, and greeted Marco like a long-lost brother. Marco was, as always, courteous, but his manner lacked warmth. The older man's obsequiousness disgusted him, and Harriet sensed it, even if her father didn't.

Also unaware was his wife. Harriet saw that the wicked step-mother had vanished. In her place was a thin, brittle little woman, suddenly anxious to proclaim her connection to a stepdaughter she'd previously despised.

Only Olympia behaved normally, cheeking Marco like a younger sister, embracing Lucia and Harriet, teasing everyone out of their unease.

As more guests arrived and Guiseppe d'Estino's attention was taken up with greeting them, Harriet took her sister aside, resisting Olympia's efforts to escape.

'Darling I'm joint hostess, I really have a lot to do—'

'You can do it when you've spent some time with me, little sister. Why does our father act as though he's only just found out about my engagement?'

'Because he has. That phone message you left for him when you arrived never reached him. Mamma made sure of that.'

'But you knew at Manelli's party,' Harriet said. 'Didn't you—?'

'No, I didn't tell him, because I didn't want him madder at me than he was already. He was furious when I turned Marco down. The title, you see.'

'But it's not Marco's title.'

'Darling, he's a count's nephew. Pappa's a snob, and Mamma's even worse. I really must be going, someone's calling me—'

She danced away, leaving Harriet to digest what she'd read between the lines. Guiseppe wanted Marco in the family as the husband of his favourite daughter, but Olympia wouldn't oblige. Then he'd remembered that Harriet was also his child, so she would have to do instead. She'd even been promoted to favourite off-spring, now that she could be useful.

The party was in full swing. Her father made much of her, but even more of Marco, some-times asking the same question several times when he ran out of inspiration. After her first severity of disappointment Harriet found herself feeling sorry for him. She was also growing more and more embarrassed to be introduced to people as, 'My daughter Harriet, engaged to *Count* Calvani's nephew.'

Just when she thought things couldn't get any worse, they did. Guiseppe launched into a speech about what a wonderful time 'my dear child' would have at the two weddings in Venice the following week. He would be thinking of her, he said repeatedly, and she must remember him to Count Calvani, 'an old and dear friend'. Harriet grew cold with shame as it dawned on her that her father was hinting for an invitation to the weddings. So that was why this meeting couldn't have waited.

She hardly dared look at Marco, but when she did his face was frozen into a mask of courtesy. At the first possible moment he excused himself and moved away. She wished the earth would open and swallow her up. Luckily Signor Carnelli was there, and he claimed her attention.

At the back of the house was a large, well-stocked conservatory, where several of the older guests had settled to talk. Seeing his mother, Marco drifted to the entrance where, from the other side of a bank of ferns, he heard a female voice, lofty, imperious.

'An extraordinary young woman, and more English than Italian, despite her name. Frankly, Lucia, I wonder at you promoting such a match for your son. Harriet lacks finish, and she'll never really be one of us.'

A hush fell as Marco appeared and stood there, taking the measure of the woman. She was the Baroness d'Alari, thin-faced, cold-eyed, a woman who made up in pride and spite what she lacked in almost everything else. The discovery that Marco had heard her made her fall silent, but from chagrin, not shame.

'I suppose it didn't occur to you, Baroness,' he said, 'that my fiancée isn't trying to be one of anything? She is unique, a brave, original woman, with a style—and a mind—of her own. In short, she is exactly what I wish her to be.'

It was years since anyone had snubbed the Baroness, and she had no resources to cope.

'I suppose it's natural that you should defend her,' she snapped, 'but beware defending her too rudely, young man. I believe my husband is one of your more important clients.'

'All my clients are important, and you must forgive me if I decline to discuss that matter with anyone but your husband,' Marco said, anger glinting in his dark eyes. 'If he wishes to take his business elsewhere, doubtless he will inform me. There are several other establishments where he will be gladly received. Excuse me.'

As he moved away Lucia rose and came after

him, tucking her hand into his arm. 'Well done, my dear boy! I never could stand that woman,' she said happily. 'The perfect end to a perfect evening.'

'You're not leaving already?'

'Yes, I'm a little tired. The chauffeur will take me home, and you can bring Harriet on later.'

'I think she'll need to talk to you. I'm sure she's seen the truth about tonight.'

'Certain to. She blinded herself because she wanted to feel she still had a father, but she's too intelligent to blind herself for long. Awful, snobbish little man! How Etta produced him I'll never know. But the person she'll need to talk to is you.'

'Mamma—what can I say to her—?'

'My son, if you don't know how to comfort her when she's unhappy, I can only say that it's time you found out.'

'I'll do my best.'

'Marco,' she said anxiously, 'how are things between you and Harriet?'

He shrugged. 'What can I tell you? She blows hot and cold. Sometimes I think she disapproves of me.'

'Nonsense, how could she?'

He grinned, briefly boyish and delightful.

'There speaks my mother.' He kissed her cheek. 'Goodnight Mamma.'

The evening seemed to stretch endlessly ahead of Harriet. When Lucia said goodbye she wished she could have gone with her, but it was too soon. Lucia had the excuse of age, but her own early departure would be insulting.

Then Marco appeared beside her, carrying a much needed cup of coffee. 'Bear up. I promise I'll get you away soon.'

'Was I that obvious?' she said, accepting the cup gratefully.

'You were looking as if you'd had enough.'

'Oh, dear, I hope I haven't offended any of your important business contacts.'

'No, I did that. But it was worth it. I'll tell you another time.'

'Marco, my dear boy!' It was her father, clapping him on the shoulder. 'I've just said goodbye to your excellent mother. I understand, of course, that she needs to save her energy for the journey to Venice next week. Weddings can be so tiring, especially large weddings. Why I'll bet they can't even keep track of all the people they've invited—'

Unable to stand any more, Harriet slipped away, leaving Marco in her father's clutches. She felt bad about that but she was ready to scream.

After an hour she found Marco beside her again. 'That wasn't very kind, but I don't blame you,' he said. 'Come on, we're leaving. Unless you'd prefer to stay.'

'Get me out of here,' she said with feeling.

It took nearly another hour to make their farewells, and Guiseppe walked with them to the car, talking non-stop. But at last they were on their way.

Harriet slumped silently in her seat as the car swung out of Rome headed for the Appian Way. Finally she roused herself.

'You knew, didn't you?' she said. 'You knew as soon as you heard about the invitation. That's what you were trying to warn me last night.'

'I guessed there was a reason why he'd suddenly decided to remember that he was your father. I'm sorry. That was a sad business for you.'

The words were kind but he didn't take her hand and his eyes were fixed on the road.

When they stopped outside the villa he said, 'I won't come in. I have to be getting back to my paperwork. Goodnight.'

'Goodnight,' she said huskily, and ran into the house and up the stairs. She wanted to be alone, and at the same time she wanted someone to be there. But there was no comfort to be found in Marco, and the sooner she finished with him the better.

In her room she tossed her bag aside and put her tiara back in its box. She stood at the window in the moonlight, feeling lonely and bleak. Tonight something had been taken from her that she knew she would never get back. It might have been a pointless hope, but she'd clung to it, and now it was over. Gradually she lost track of time and had no idea how long she'd been standing there when she heard the knock at her door. Outside she found Marco. He'd discarded his jacket and bow-tie, and was holding a vacuum jug and a mug.

'I brought you something you need,' he said, easing his way past her. 'English tea.'

He set the mug down and poured out the tea, already milked. It was exactly as she liked it.

'This was a wonderful idea. Thank you.'

She sat down on the bed, and he sat beside her. She met his eyes and found them very dark and kind.

'I thought you'd gone,' she said.

'I changed my mind. I came into the house and waited for you to come back downstairs. I thought you might need to talk. When you didn't return I—well, maybe I'm starting to understand you by now. I still reckoned you might need someone to listen. I'm quite good at that.'

'Thank you for coming,' she said softly. 'But there's nothing to say, is there? I've had something confirmed that I suppose I always knew. I should have faced it years ago. I thought I had. More fool me.'

'You're not going to make the mistake of minding what he says or does, are you?' Marco chided her gently.

'No, of course not. After all, he was saying all the right things, making a fuss of me, just as I always dreamed. Only—it wasn't me he was making a fuss of. It was you. He's just a petty snob. As he sees it I've snared myself a count's nephew, so suddenly I'm his daughter again.'

'Harriet, stop this,' he urged. 'You're a fine woman, beautiful, brainy and strong. You've built an independent life on your own talents. You don't need him. You never did.'

'I know, I know. It's silly isn't it?' Suddenly tears were pouring down her cheeks and she set the mug down hurriedly as her control deserted her. 'Why should it matter after all this time? I'm not a child any more.'

She finished on a husky sob and at once his arms were about her, holding her firmly in the comforting embrace her father had never given her.

'In a way you are,' he murmured against her

hair. 'Your childhood is never really over. Its ghosts haunt you all your life.'

She clung to him, unable to stop crying now she'd started. The grief of years poured out and she could do nothing but yield to it.

'He never loved me,' she choked, 'not really.'

'He did at the start. Remember what you told me, how you two adored each other?'

'Not even then. If he'd really loved me he couldn't just have discarded me like that, could he?'

'I don't know,' he sighed. 'Some people love that way. Real enough at the time, but shallow. Others—do it differently.' He laid his cheek against her hair and held her again, saying, 'I'm here, I'm here,' as another paroxysm shook her.

She tried to speak but she couldn't get the words out coherently.

'What is it?' he asked gently, cupping her face and turning it up so that he could see her better. 'Tell me.'

'Nothing,' she choked, 'I'm all right now.'

'I don't think you are.' He took out a clean handkerchief and dabbed her wet cheeks. Her hair was coming down over his hands.

'What do I look like?' she asked shakily.

'Like a little girl who's just found out her father doesn't love her. But you won't give in to despair. You know the world still has much for you.'

'I don't know what the world holds for me,' she said huskily. 'Right now I'm not really sure that I care.'

'Never speak like that again,' he said sternly. 'I forbid it. Only weaklings say it doesn't matter what happens, and you are strong, *cara*. You're the kind of person who wrests life to your will.'

He looked down into her face for a moment, then he lowered his head and laid his lips on hers, keeping them still for a moment, then moving them very slowly. It was the lightest of touches, but it was enough to bring her to instant, eager life. Her own mouth began to move in helpless response, urging and encouraging him.

He had a moment of doubt, enough to make him raise his head and give her a troubled look. He'd come to her bedroom offering comfort, but not of this kind. Harriet saw the 'man of honour' in his eyes, threatening to restrain him.

She dealt with that man swiftly, slipping her hand behind Marco's head and drawing him back down to where her warm, persuasive lips could tell him, without words, what she wanted. Now she was ready for him, her lips already parted, welcoming the entry of his questing tongue. The signal she'd given him had taken the brakes off his control and his fevered movements were telling her that now he felt free to do whatever he liked.

Good!

His tongue teased her own before starting a lazy exploration of her mouth. Her response was electric. No other kiss had ever been so thrilling, and it wasn't enough. Now she had to have him in every possible way.

His mouth drifted down her neck and across her chest, and she drew in a long, shaking breath. It felt shatteringly good to have his lips there, where she'd so often longed to feel them, tracing the swell of one breast while his fingers outlined the other. Her neckline was low, but not low enough for him, for he made a sound of impatience at the resistance of the material. The next moment she heard the sound of tearing, felt the shock of cool air, and her breasts were free. Instantly she sensed all constraint fell away from her, as though her spirit too had flown free. This was the man she wanted. She wanted his love, and she wanted his passion, and she vowed to herself that if she couldn't have one she was going to have the other.

He dropped his head between her breasts, rejoicing in their silkiness with his tongue, while his hand celebrated their shape with joy. Wherever he touched her the result was electric, sending shivers of sensation everywhere, along her arms, her legs, between her thighs.

The dress was torn to just below her breasts. As his fingers curled around the edge he met her glowing eyes. Reading consent in them, he tightened his hand and wrenched hard, ripping the dress open to the hem, revealing the whole length of her body. Half dazed she reached up for him, pulling at his black bow-tie, then the buttons of his shirt. He finished the job himself, tossing aside his clothes and pulling her against him while the remainder of her ruined dress slipped to the floor.

She wished the light was better, so that she could see him, but there was only the sensation of his nakedness pressed against hers, his hands exploring her intimately with slow, sensual movements that made her vibrantly aware in every inch of her own body.

She began her own exploration of him, discovering that his shoulders really were as broad as they seemed in an elegant dinner jacket, his spine as long and supple, his hips as narrow. Through her wild, whirling thoughts she promised herself that soon they would do this again, and she would know him better, know the caresses he liked and that provoked him. Meantime, she was learning and it was wonderful.

His fingers were on the soft insides of her thighs, making teasing promises that drove her half out of her mind. A long, soft moan broke from her and he moved slightly so that he could look into her wild face on the pillow, her magnificent hair spread out.

She thought she whispered his name, she wasn't sure, but the next moment he was between her thighs, skilfully urging her to greater and greater passion until she was ready for the moment he entered her. And then everything was right, and perfect. Everything was as it was always meant to be, and she was a part of it for ever.

He moved strongly inside her, and while she felt the pleasure mounting she was aware that his hands were touching her face softly. She would hardly have believed he could be so tender but each caress was unbelievably gentle, so unlike the Marco who dominated his world, but hinting at the man she was sure lived deep inside him. And she could coax that man out, she was sure of it, just as he was reaching out to her now...

Then all thought was shut off as the pleasure took her over, shook her until she seemed to dissolve. The world flew apart into a million pieces, that flamed in the universe before drifting back together and reforming into a world that was no longer the same, would never be the same again.

She tried to speak but Marco's fingertips were across her lips, his arms about her, his lips against her hair, murmuring reassurances. A heavy languor seemed to weigh her down until she fell into a deep sleep with his arms still about her.

As she dozed in the early morning she felt a slight disturbance in the bed next to her. Opening her eyes a crack she saw Marco rise and stand a moment in the grey light. Last night she'd felt his body but seen little of it. Now she saw him fully, the long legs, lean but with muscular thighs, the narrow hips with their unmistakable power. She remembered that power, how he'd used it to drive her to an ecstasy whose memory melted her again now. If he had reached for her, she would be his again.

Instead he dressed quickly, while she lay listening to the rustling movements, waiting for the moment when he would awaken her to say goodbye. Or perhaps he would simply kiss her, and she could put her arms about him. But then the movements stopped, and there was a long silence. She opened her eyes to see him standing in the window, his head sunk on his chest, the picture of a deeply troubled man. He seemed to be staring at the inner distance and seeing something there that disturbed him.

At last he straightened his shoulders and seemed to give himself a little shake, as though discarding thoughts that were no use to him. Then he walked out of the door.

CHAPTER TEN

THREE days later they all flew to Venice, Harriet and Lucia departing from the villa, and Marco going from his apartment and meeting them at Rome airport.

'Are you sure you're not sickening for something?' Lucia asked Harriet anxiously as they drove to the airport. 'You're very pale, and you've been quiet the last couple of days.'

'I just don't enjoy flying,' Harriet put her off.

It was true that she'd been quiet ever since the moment she'd seen her lover leave in the dawn, and lain there, aching with desolation.

She acquitted him of deliberate unkindness. She would never forget that he'd returned to the house to comfort her, how gently he'd spoken, and how much understanding he'd shown. He'd felt with her, as only a truly sensitive man could have done, and she would always love him for it.

In the moments of passion, too, he'd treated her with great tenderness. But then he'd left her alone in a way that felt nothing less than brutal.

The next day Lucia had told her excitedly of
Marco's encounter with the Baroness d'Alari,
and the way he'd risked losing valuable business to defend her. That too warmed her heart,
but it cooled again when she realised that he
wasn't going to tell her himself.

She could sympathise with the wariness that
made him shrink from too much human contact.
She could even pity him for it. But she increasingly felt that she couldn't live with it.

A resolution had formed in her, to leave as
soon as possible after the wedding. It would
break her heart, but the misery would be short-
lived, unlike the misery of being married to a
man who would allow himself to get close to
her only to withdraw as though she'd turned
into an enemy.

With the decision taken she pushed it aside
until after the coming weddings, determined not
to spoil them for anyone else. At Rome airport
she greeted Marco with cool composure, and a
smile that gave away no more than did his own.
This was her first trip to Venice, and she was
going to enjoy it. She could be wretched later.

The Calvani family began to gather in Venice
two days before the first wedding. The Rome
party arrived to find Guido and Dulcie waiting
for them with two motor boats to take them
across the lagoon, one driven by Guido himself.

'You're lucky he's not trying to take you in a gondola,' Dulcie chuckled, referring to their early courtship when she'd thought he was a gondolier, and he'd let her go on believing it, thinking that he was luring her into his net, while actually he was the one being lured.

The Palazzo Calvani was a treasure trove of masterpieces and Harriet soon settled to explore it in the company of the count's archivist, who had been put at her disposal.

Leo turned up next day, looking less cheerful than Harriet remembered. She and Dulcie were both fond of him, and it took them no time to divine his trouble. Settling on the big sofa, one each side of him, they went onto the attack.

'You've found her at last,' Harriet said.

He played dumb. 'Her?'

She thumped his shoulder. 'You know what I mean. *Her!* The one.' Remembering that he was at heart a cowboy she added, 'She's got you roped and tied.'

'What's her name?' Dulcie demanded.

'Selena. I met her in Texas. We stayed at the same ranch after she had an accident with her horse trailer.'

He fell silent.

'And?' they asked, in an agony of impatience.

'We practised for the rodeo together.'

'*And?*'

'She fell off. So did I. Mind you, she only fell off in the practise ring, and I did it in front of a crowd of thousands. But we both fell off.'

'So you started with something in common,' Dulcie said wisely.

'A marriage of true minds,' Harriet agreed.

'I shouldn't think minds had much to do with it,' Dulcie observed, recalling certain tales Guido had told her about Leo.

'Nothing at all,' Leo sighed like a man remembering bliss. 'It was wonderful.'

Harriet's lips twitched as she met Dulcie's eyes, equally full of mirth.

'You should have brought her here to meet us,' she said.

'That's just the trouble, I don't know where to find her.'

'But didn't you exchange names and addresses?' Dulcie asked.

'Yes, but—' He plunged into a long account of the troubles that had separated him from his true love, finishing gloomily, 'I might never see her again.'

A cry of, 'Hey, Leo!' made him drift off to join the other men. Dulcie and Harriet refused to meet each other's eyes, but at last they couldn't stand it, and burst out laughing.

'Oh, we mustn't,' Harriet said, conscience stricken. 'We're terrible to laugh.'

'I know,' Dulcie choked. 'But I can't help it. Did you ever hear such a crazy story?'

Harriet shook her head. 'Poor Leo. It could only happen to him.'

The next day they all gathered in the small side chapel of St Mark's Basilica, for the wedding of Count Calvani to his beloved Liza. The count's three nephews were groomsmen, and Liza was attended by the three ladies.

The reception was a strange affair. Despite her new status Liza was first and foremost a housewife who'd spent the last three months organising Dulcie and Guido's wedding, set for next day. This was a big society occasion, with enough guests to fill the glorious St Mark's Basilica, followed by a huge reception at the Palazzo Calvani which she insisted on overseeing in every detail.

She lingered at her own reception long enough for her devoted groom to toast her, then hurried off to the kitchens, for 'a quick look.' At last Count Francesco yielded to the inevitable and followed her.

'I don't think she appreciates her good fortune at all,' Lucia said in bafflement. 'She treats him really badly.'

'That may be the secret,' Guido said with a

grin. 'After all the women who put themselves out to catch his eye, the one he loves is the one who makes him fight for her attention.'

After that the party broke up into couples. Guido and Dulcie wandered away, arms about each other. Leo and Lucia settled down for a long comfortable talk in the moonlit garden, and Marco said abruptly to Harriet, 'Shall we take a walk?'

Venice at night, a city of dark alleys leading to mystery, half-lights, ancient stones, shadows. The faint sound of music reached them, inter-mingled with the haunting cries of gondoliers echoing back and forth through the tiny canals. They strolled in silence for a while, walking apart.

'I thought we should talk,' he said.

'It's time,' she agreed.

'Watching that wedding service today made me do a lot of thinking. You, too, I expect.'

'Oh, yes,' she mused. 'A lot.'

'They say one wedding begets another. Don't you realise how people are looking at us, ex-pecting us to name the day?'

'I had noticed the odd significant look.'

'Tomorrow might be a good time.'

'A time for—?' she asked cautiously.

'To announce a wedding date. We've had enough time to make a decision. My own decision is made. I did a wise thing when I came to London to find you. And you're a natural Roman, anyone can see that. You're even building up a clientele. When you move your business here you'll have the basics already. We make a perfect team.'

'Looked at like that, I suppose we do,' she mused.

'So can I tell my mother that it's settled?' he asked briskly.

This was it? This was a proposal of marriage in the softly lit alleys of Venice, with the stars glowing up above, and the atmosphere of romance all around? She didn't know whether to laugh or cry.

'I don't think we should rush a decision,' she said at last. 'You say I'm suitable because I'm a natural Roman and because I've already started to build up a clientele. That's a pretty narrow list of qualifications for a wife. Also, there's something that's never been mentioned between us, and perhaps it should be.'

'I was waiting for you to speak about it,' he said. 'That night we spent together—came as quite a surprise.'

'You mean because you were the first man I'd slept with? Does it matter?'

'It took me completely by surprise. You're twenty-seven, and these days—'

'I know. But most men have always bored me after a short time, even the ones I briefly thought I fancied. When it came to the point, there was always something more interesting to do, and they never seemed to stick around to try to persuade me.'

'Can you blame them for losing heart once they realised they were competing with the Emperor Augustus?'

'I suppose not.'

They walked on and found themselves at the edge of St Mark's Square, which was emptying fast. At the outdoor cafés the chairs were being put on tables and the orchestras had fallen silent, all but one solitary violinist still playing for a couple dancing in the piazza, lost in each other.

'I thought we were reasonably good together,' he said. 'Didn't you?'

The warmth of his breath on her face, his body entwined with hers, urging, compelling, imploring, the hot, dark madness of him inside her. Reasonably good together.

'Oh, yes,' she said wryly, 'the experiment was a success in every way. Optimum results.'

Take me in your arms and dance with me under the stars, to a lone violin.

'I think things have gone well since the day

you arrived. The best day is the first Saturday in September.'

The violin stopped.

'You've fixed the date without consulting me?'

'Not fixed, but I've been thinking of suitable dates. I've got some big deals going down.'

'All your deals are big,' she mused, playing for time.

'But these are different. They'll make me. It'll be a partnership.'

'And that's what you really want, more than anything in the world?'

He gave a little embarrassed laugh. 'Not just that. I'd be the youngest partner the bank's ever had. Maybe it's a kind of vanity, but it would please me. This will take all my attention for the next few weeks. By the time I can raise my head it will be September, and the summer will be over unless we make our plans now.'

'No, Marco stop it. I won't be rushed.'

'But it's common sense—'

'Listen,' she said desperately. 'Do you remember what you said to me in the *Bella Figura*? You said, "Control is the answer. If you're not in control, somebody else is. So you must always be the one in control." I didn't know then how true it was. Even with me.'

'You're reading more into that than it'll take. One of us has to plan ahead.'

'You're planning too far ahead for me. I'm sorry, but I'm just not sure about marriage.'

'But you just said—'

'Sometimes optimum results aren't enough.'

'Well, what *will* be enough?'

'I don't know, but the jury's still out. I don't know what my future plans are.'

'You don't mean—' he was peering at her in the semi darkness '—that you're actually thinking of leaving?'

'Not leaving Rome, just your home. There are some nice apartments on the Via del—'

He drew a sharp breath. 'You've been looking at apartments?'

'Only in the newspapers.'

'You've got it all worked out, haven't you?' he said coldly. 'May I ask when you were going to tell me?'

'Not until after we'd left here. And I still haven't quite decided.'

'So until you do I'm supposed to bide my time and be a suppliant, waiting on your pleasure? Perhaps I don't like that?'

'And perhaps I don't like your assumption that since *you've* made your decision *I* have to jump to it. There are two decisions to be made here, Marco. Not just yours.'

He turned away, striding up and down on the flagstones. Harriet could sense his irritation at having his plans frustrated.

'Maybe people who fight as much as we do shouldn't think of marriage,' she suggested. 'Let's leave it there for tonight, or we'll really quarrel.'

'All right. Let's leave it there.'

They walked back through the little streets, where the ghosts of a thousand lovers lingered, whispering to those who had ears to hear. But these two passed on without a backward glance. When they came to the side entrance to the Palazzo Calvani they slipped indoors, bid each other a courteous goodnight, and went their separate ways.

One by one, the lights were going out along the Grand Canal. In the garden Leo rose and helped Lucia to her feet.

'Thank you for listening to my ramblings,' he said. 'I'm afraid Dulcie and Harriet thought me a bit of a clown.'

'Well, your life has been rather full of entanglements,' Lucia said, patting his hand. 'But if Selena is the right woman, you'll find her again. Although I think she's quite mad if *she* doesn't come to find *you*.'

'Maybe she doesn't want to find me,' Leo said gloomily.

'Enough of that kind of talk,' Lucia said severely. 'If your love is fated to be, it will be. Now, tomorrow's a wedding. We're all going to enjoy ourselves.'

Dulcie and Guido said goodnight outside her bedroom.

'Can't I come in, just for a moment?' he whispered.

'Not the night before the wedding. It isn't proper.'

'Proper? Hang it Dulcie, after what we've been doing whenever we got the chance—? No, don't laugh like that. It does things to me. I may lose all control.'

She kissed him tenderly. 'Go to bed and dream of me.'

'I always dream of you. Do you love me?'

'More than life. More than all the world.'

'There are no words to say how much I love you,' he whispered. 'Goodnight heart of my heart, until tomorrow, when I shall make you mine.'

'Now leave the work,' Francesco commanded his new countess as she took a last look around the great kitchens. 'It's time my bride stopped neglecting me and kissed me instead.'

'Your bride,' she whispered. 'After so long.'

'After too long, beloved.'

He took both her hands and gazed into her face, seeing not the lines, but the beautiful candour with which she'd first looked at him, forty-five years ago.

Liza smiled back. For her too the signs of age were invisible, and he was the young lion she'd first worshipped in those long-ago days when she'd been a kitchen maid and any thought of marriage had seemed hopeless. But through long years he'd loved her steadfastly, perhaps not always faithfully, but, she would have argued, who could blame him for that when she kept turning him down?

She rested her head against him. 'I'm sorry *caro*, but how could I neglect the preparation for tomorrow? It's the big wedding.'

'Oh, no,' he said, drawing her firmly away from the kitchen. 'Today was the big wedding. Come, my adored one...'

Dulcie was a traditional bride, glowing in white satin and lace, wearing the Calvani pearls for the first time. She looked serenely happy, while Guido looked as if he was taking something seriously for the first time in his life, according to Marco.

Marco and Leo were the groomsmen, Marco impeccably dressed and stylish, Leo occasionally running a finger around the inside of his formal collar.

Last night's reception had been confined to the family, at Liza's wish. This one was a glittering affair, spreading through most of the great *palazzo*. Light poured out of every door and window and gleamed from the jewellery of several hundred woman. The cream of Italian society was here.

Despite what she'd said the night before Harriet was wearing her engagement ring, not wanting to attract attention today. Dancing in Marco's arms, she played her role of the happy fiancée, and gradually realised that it was as he'd said. People were smiling at them significantly.

She'd dressed more sedately than had been her habit in company recently. This was the bride's day, so her gown was a demure olive-green silk, cut with extreme elegance and simplicity.

'Did I tell you that you look wonderful?' Marco said. 'I'm proud of you.'

The music seemed to be flowing through her veins, making her dip and sway as though there were no problems in the world. Thankfully his annoyance of last night hadn't carried over to today. He'd performed his wedding duties charmingly, and smiled through the first few dances before holding out his hand to Harriet in a silent invitation.

Dulcie, watching them, signalled to the band who promptly broke into a popular song called 'See How He Loves You'. The crowd cheered, thinking of the bride and groom who were dancing together, holding each other close, but Dulcie mischievously pointed a finger at Marco and Harriet.

Despite her resolution to be sensible she found herself responding to Marco's nearness, his arms about her, the closeness of his face to hers. Their last embrace had been in her bed, naked, limbs entwined, exchanging pleasure. The dance was like a teasing echo of that time, a reminder, a promise...

At this moment it was easy to believe that nothing else mattered. Warmth seemed to enfold her, his warmth, her own, welling up from deep inside her in response to him. The handsome face near hers was the face she loved, the dark eyes gentle, glowing, silently telling her that he too was thinking...

That was how they communicated best, she

realised, in silence. And surely they could find a way forward to a future together?

As the dance ended people crowded around them, laughing expectantly.

'Come on, tell us…'

'Time you set the date…'

Marco's arm was still about her waist. Harriet felt it tighten suddenly.

'We've set the date,' he said. 'The first Saturday in September.'

Her gasp of shock was drowned in the cheers. The Calvani men pressed forward, shaking Marco's hands, Lucia beamed, Dulcie threw her arms around Harriet, squealing, 'I'm so glad, I'm so glad.'

'That's great!' Guido yelled. 'I can't wait to see this. I suppose we are invited?' he clowned.

To everyone's astonishment Marco clowned back. 'Dulcie is, you're not.'

A roar of laughter went up at this very moderate joke which sounded like a major witticism coming from such an unexpected source.

'Kiss her,' somebody yelled. 'Kiss the bride!'

Harriet felt as though the ground had shattered beneath her. One moment she'd been dazed to the point of granting Marco anything, the next he'd given her a grandstand display of everything about him that antagonised her. It was as though the temperature had dropped to freezing in a split second and she was in a new world, bleak, unforgiving. As unforgiving as her own heart.

She let him kiss her. There was no choice in this gathering. What she had to say must wait.

But waiting meant enduring the count's delighted insistence that the wedding must take place in Venice, at the family home. It meant watching Lucia put her head together with Liza, making plans. She didn't know how she got through the next hour.

Lucia's joy was the hardest to bear. She made it clear that she loved Harriet, and nothing would make her happier than to see her married to her son. Harriet tried to give her a hint.

'He shouldn't have done it like that,' she said desperately. 'Announcing it to the world before telling you, but you see we're not—'

'Oh, my dear, I understand. You can't blame Marco if his feelings ran away with him. Besides, he told me last night.'

'He did what?'

'Just before you went out together, he said he'd been thinking of that Saturday, and he would finalise it with you.'

'And what did he say when he returned?' Harriet asked, her eyes kindling.

'I was asleep by then, and of course today has been so hectic I haven't even had the chance to tell you how pleased I am.' She kissed her cheek. 'Now we're all going to be so happy.'

She fluttered away, unaware that she'd filled Harriet's heart with anger and dismay.

The cake had been eaten, the bride and groom had slipped away, the band played its last number.

'My uncle asks that you join the rest of the family in saying goodbye to our guests,' Marco told her. 'He considers you one of us.'

She turned smouldering eyes on him. 'I wouldn't hurt your uncle for the world,' she said. 'But you and I have to talk.'

'There'll be time for that later. I know how it looks, but just be patient.'

His hand on her arm urged her away. The count made her stand beside him, his wife on the other side. It was a place of honour, but it also showed her how fast the net was closing about her.

When the last guest had gone she took firm hold of Marco.

'*Now!*' she said.

He let her draw him into the next room. 'Let me talk first,' he said.

'You've talked enough. Now you'll listen. How dare you do that! I told you last night that I wasn't ready for this. Didn't you hear me?'

'Yes, I heard you, but you didn't make any

sense. Harriet, you know as well as I do that you're going to say yes eventually. We've both known that ever since—well, for some time. Why drag it out? All right, we fight sometimes, but we also go well together.'

'We don't go well together, because I could never ''go well'' with a man who rolls over me like a juggernaut.'

'All right, I'm sorry for the way I did it, but can't we put that behind us—?'

'And then do what? Go on where? To a wedding? Marco, I'm further from marrying you now than I've ever been. Please think about that before you make any more plans without consulting me.'

She walked away from him and up the stairs to her room. She had never been so angry in her life.

CHAPTER ELEVEN

MARCO'S secretary looked in alarm at the determined young woman who stood before her.

'Does Signor Calvani have anyone with him just now?'

'I don't see what—?'

'Does he?' Harriet repeated.

'No, but he has a board meeting in five—'

'Don't worry, I won't be that long,' she tossed over her shoulder as she opened the door to Marco's office.

He was engrossed in a computer screen and looked up in alarm.

'What's wrong? Has something happened to my mother?'

'No, I came to see you because this is the one place you can't run from me. You've been avoiding me since we returned from Venice.'

'Two days. You know I have work to do—'

'And you know what I want to say. I'll say it quickly so that you're not late for your meeting.'

His lips tightened. 'This isn't the time—'

'How much time does it take to say good-bye?'

'Can we talk about this later?'

'No, I fell for that one before. Not again. Besides, there's nothing to talk about. Goodbye! Finito. *Basta!* End of story. I can't marry you. This so-called engagement is over.'

'Don't be absurd,' he said impatiently. 'The invitations have started to go out.'

'And I'm upsetting the organisation, the ultimate crime, I know. I'm sorry, but some things are more important than getting the books straight.'

Marco came out from behind his desk. He was pale but he spoke calmly. 'Look, you've been in a strange mood recently, and maybe I haven't been very sympathetic. And I shouldn't have announced our engagement like that, but it just seemed the right thing to do. I'm sorry. I'll do better in future.'

'Listen to yourself,' she cried. 'You talk like a man punching keys on a computer. This one for ''sorry'', this one for ''do better'', and out comes the right answer. Life doesn't work like that.'

He made a sound of impatience. 'Do these trivial details matter?'

'They're not trivial. They're the way you are. Everything labelled and in its little box. I've just told you that our engagement is off, and you're angry because I've stepped out of my box into one you don't know how to label.'

'I'm angry because I don't understand a word of this. Nothing you say is reasonable.'

'Is it unreasonable of me to want to marry a man who cares about me, the way you don't?'

He took a quick breath and seemed about to say something, but checked himself. When the words did come out they were calm. 'I thought we'd—managed to grow closer—'

'Not close enough. You're possessive, and you try to organise every step I take, but that isn't love.' She sighed. 'Well, maybe you're right and I have been unreasonable. I should have worried about love much sooner, shouldn't I? Like, the day we met. I'm sorry. I didn't know myself very well then. I do now, and different things matter. Love matters.'

'Love?' he echoed.

'Oh, Marco, you sound as though you'd never heard the word. There's no love between us, is there?'

He was very still now. She had his whole attention. 'It would seem not,' he said quietly. 'How stupid of me not to have understood.'

'It's my fault. I misled you, made you think I could live without it, like you.'

He regarded her sardonically. 'And when did this suddenly become so important?'

'Only recently. Do you remember the night of my father's party?'

'Do *you?*' he flashed unexpectedly.

'Vividly. But it's no good is it? You can't create what isn't there. I've tried to play it your way, but I can't do it, and it would only break us apart in the end.'

'Maybe you give up too easily.'

'I thought you prided yourself on being a realist. You're not being realistic now. It's not going to get any better, Marco. We're both what we are. It's too late to change.'

She watched his face, longing to see in it some softening, some hint that even now he could search his heart and discover that he didn't want to lose her. Behind her brave front she knew that a loving word from him would have sent her joyfully into his arms. But no word came.

Instead, into her mind slid the memory of something he'd said in one of their discussions about business, 'It's like playing poker. When the deal collapses you keep a blank face.'

The deal was collapsing and his face was as blank as death. His complexion was even a little grey, and there was a strange, withered look in his eyes, as though the life was draining out of him.

'Yes,' he said at last in a voice of stone. 'It's too late for change. I thought—well, I was wrong. You can't change just because you want to.'

In the silence that followed she had the strange feeling that he was at a loss, something she'd never known in him before.

'What happens now?' he asked at last.

'I'll leave as soon as I've spoken to your mother. When I get back to London—'

'London? You were talking about staying in Rome.'

She surveyed him ironically. 'You actually remember that conversation? I thought you pressed the ''Delete'' button the way you do when something doesn't suit you. I did mean to stay in Rome, but I see now that I can't. I have to get right away from you. When I'm home I'll arrange to repay the money I owe you.'

'There's no rush. I promised you easy terms—'

'No, I want to pay it all at once.'

'You can't afford a lump sum, we both know that.'

'I'll manage it somehow. It's better if I'm not in your debt.'

Suddenly his face wasn't impassive any

more, but twisted with bitterness. 'You can't wait to be rid of me, can you?'

The injustice was like a knife in her heart, making her reply with equal bitterness to cover her pain.

'I thought you'd be glad to see me gone, now that you know the proposed merger isn't coming off. Cut your losses and don't waste time over a dead deal. Your own principles, but useful for me, too.'

She heard the quick intake of breath before he said, 'I seem to have taught you more than I knew. I can recall a time when you were too generous to say something so cruel.'

'Marco—'

'You're quite right of course. Whatever made me think it worthy of discussion?'

'Nothing is worth discussing any more. It's over. There's no more to be said. You'd better hurry, you have a meeting.'

She almost ran out of his office, not knowing whether to cry or hurl something at him. How dare he confuse her with that air of suppressed pain! She knew him too well to be fooled. It was no more than his trick of putting her in the wrong. But right now she couldn't cope with it.

Telling Lucia was the hardest part, although the older woman was understanding.

'I always knew there was something wrong,' she sighed. 'Even in Venice I sensed it. But I suppose I saw only what I wanted to see. I'm afraid Marco gets that from me.' She squeezed Harriet's hand. 'What happened?'

'It's very simple. Marco and I made a business deal, but I found I couldn't stick to the terms. My feelings got all tangled up, the very thing we agreed wouldn't happen.'

'But he wants you so much—'

'Yes, he wants me, as he'd want anything that he'd decided suited him. But it's not enough.'

'Are you saying that you love him?'

'It's not as simple as that,' she said, on her guard, remembering that Lucia would probably report all this to her son. 'How can you love a man who doesn't need to be loved?'

'Every man needs to be loved, and Marco perhaps more than the others, because he fights it so hard.'

'Yes, he fights it, and I can't get past that. I don't want to spend my life fighting.'

'Can't I say anything to persuade you?'

Harriet shook her head. 'The hardest thing will be leaving you. You've been wonderful to me.'

'We mustn't lose that,' Lucia said eagerly.

'Now that we've found each other you must promise to stay in touch.'

Harriet promised, and the older woman put her arms around her. There were tears in her eyes. 'When will you leave?' she asked sadly.

'There's a plane at noon tomorrow.'

'I'll go to the airport with you.'

Harriet was half inclined to leave behind her new clothes. It didn't seem right somehow to take from a woman she was disappointing so badly. But Lucia insisted that every last gown was packed.

'Cara Etta,' she said earnestly, 'Forgive me for saying this, but I couldn't bear for you to go back to looking as you did before.'

Over supper they tried to cheer each other up, and not admit that they were both waiting for Marco. Lucia glanced at the clock several times until Harriet said, 'He isn't coming, you know.'

'Of course he's coming. He won't let you go without saying goodbye.'

'He doesn't need to say goodbye. He's already ''signed me off''.'

'Don't start to talk like him, my dear. That way of seeing the world hasn't made him happy.'

'I don't know what would make him happy,' Harriet sighed. 'I just don't think it's me.'

'And you?' Lucia asked. 'Could you have been happy with him?'

'Can one be happy without the other being happy?' was the only answer Harriet could make.

A heavy ache was pervading her, as though her chest housed a stone where her heart should be. As the hands of the clock ticked on she faced the fact that Marco was going to let her go without another word, and despite her defiant words about "signing off", that hurt badly.

In a fine temper, Lucia called Marco's home and then, receiving no reply, his mobile phone.

'Don't try any more,' Harriet begged. 'It's better as it is.'

Yet she still lay awake most of the night, listening for the sound of his car. When it didn't come she repeated to herself that this was the best way, for she knew she was weakening. She was in too much danger of throwing herself into his arms and promising anything if only she could stay with him. And that would be fatal. There could be no self-respect in living with a man who knew that you would abandon pride to be with him.

She managed to sleep for a couple of hours, waking with an aching head. Neither she nor Lucia had more than black coffee for breakfast. The hands of the clock were creeping to the moment when she must leave the villa for ever. Leave Marco for ever. No, she had already left him.

There was the sound from the gravel outside.

'The chauffeur must have brought the car around,' Lucia said. 'Oh, Etta dear, remember you promised to keep in touch.'

'I promise,' Harriet said huskily, and was enveloped in Lucia's embrace. Then she felt her hostess stiffen in her arms, and Lucia let out a glad cry.

'Marco!'

He was standing in the doorway, very pale but composed. Harriet held her breath.

'You came!' Lucia was overjoyed.

'Naturally. Did you think me so lacking in manners that I would allow our guest to depart without seeing her off? I'll drive Harriet to the airport myself.'

Her heart was beating strongly from the moment of blazing hope, but she forced herself to be calm. This was Marco's good manners. No more.

He waited in the car while she made her farewells to Lucia. She was still fighting back tears when she got in beside him. Marco studied her face, his own revealing little. Then his gaze dropped to her left hand, bare now.

'I didn't know you were coming,' Harriet said, so I've given me ring to your mother.'

He swung the car out on to the Appian Way. 'This has hurt my mother very much.'

'I know, but we had a long talk and I think she understands.'

'That's more than I do.'

'And I've promised to stay in touch with her.'

'Good. Then I may hope to hear some news of you.'

'What was that?' A heavy truck had passed, drowning out his words.

'I said *I may hope to hear some news of you*,' he repeated in a harsh, desperate voice.

'Yes, well—I'll be in touch about the money.'

'I've told you there's no rush for that. We can arrange instalments—'

'No, it's better to sort it all out now.'

He swore violently under his breath. 'You're a hard and stubborn woman.'

Stubborn, yes, she thought. But hard? Perhaps she was just growing a defensive shell against the pain of leaving him. It would work out for the best in the end, she told herself, especially as he was showing her his least amiable side. It really would stop hurting. One day.

At the airport he stayed with her until check-in, and politely made sure that she had her ticket, passport, boarding pass.

'I'll go straight through,' she said. 'No need to hold you up. Thank you for bringing me.'

'It was no trouble.'

'Good luck with the partnership.'

'What—? Oh, yes. Thank you. Well, I mustn't waste time. Goodbye, and the best of luck for the future.'

He shook hands with her and strode away without looking back. He found his car, got in and switched on the engine. Then he switched it off again, dropped his head on his arms on the steering wheel, and stayed like that until somebody knocked on the window to see if he was all right.

'Why did you make me seek you out here, my son?' Lucia looked around at Marco's apartment which seemed even more austere and dismaying than ever. 'It's been two days now. Why didn't you come home and talk to me?'

His smiled was strained. 'You know how busy I am just now, Mamma. This partnership—'

'You made that excuse to her, and much good it did you.'

He was silent.

Lucia went into the kitchen and made some coffee. When she returned Marco was sitting with his fingers entwined between his knees, staring at the floor. He gave a faint smile of thanks accepting the cup, and one look at his face was enough to send her back to the kitchen, returning at last with a large plate of pasta.

'When did you last eat?' she demanded, setting it before him.

He shrugged. 'Some time. Thanks Mamma.' He ate a few mouthfuls. 'This is good.'

She regarded him pityingly. 'You've been very foolish.'

'Me?' He was stung. 'I was the one who wanted our marriage to go ahead.'

'Yes, and you went about it with all the subtlety of a bludgeon. What's the result? I've lost a daughter-in-law, one I was particularly fond of. It won't do.'

'What do you expect me to do? I can't force her to marry me.'

'So you've learned that, have you?'

'Mamma it's easy to talk, but you can't talk sense to Harriet. She lives in a dream world.' He gave a grunt of sardonic laughter. 'She calls herself a businesswoman but the man in the moon has more idea of commerce. She thinks running a business is a matter of loving the pieces and finding them ''kind homes''.'

'Oh, how like Harriet that sounds!' Lucia sighed.

'Yes it does. It also sounds like the way she ran the shop into the ground. Now she talks about repaying me the money I loaned her, in a lump sum. How does she think she can do that? She's not the expert that she thinks she is.'

'Really Marco, what do you know about the subject?'

He jumped up and went to a concealed safe. A few clicks on the combination lock and he opened the door, taking out an ornate gold necklace.

'You see this? I took it to London and showed it to Harriet on the first day. Do you remember how proud Poppa was of this, how he used to show it off and tell stories of the dig where it was discovered? Harriet told me that was a fake.'

'But, my dear boy, it *is* a fake.'

'What do you mean? It's genuine Etruscan.'

'No, the original was genuine Etruscan. But years ago your father had financial problems, so he sold it. That's a copy made by a professional forger. He was the best in the business, so good that in all these years nobody has ever spotted it. Until Harriet. She, of course, could spot a phoney at fifty paces.'

He stared at her.

For the second time Harriet lifted the pen, then put it down.

'It just seems so final,' she said sadly.

Mr. Pendry, her lawyer, nodded. 'A sale *is* final,' he said. 'But you'd be very unwise to refuse Allum & Jonsey's offer.'

'But who is this firm?'

'Does it matter? A&J has met your full asking price without any argument, and as you know, I always thought it a little optimistic. Plus they want you to stay and run the place. In a sense you'll lose nothing.'

'Except that it won't be mine any more.'

'Well, if you really don't want to sell you could ask Signor Calvani if you could pay him by instalments. Shall I—?'

'No, thank you,' Harriet said firmly. He'd hit on the one argument that could sway her. She'd vowed to break all ties between herself and Marco. It was the only way to put him out of her life, if not her heart. Hell would freeze over before she asked him for a favour now. Swiftly she signed her name and pushed the paper over the desk.

'Now this one,' Mr. Pendry said. 'It's your contract, as manageress, for six months.'

Harriet paused again. 'I don't know. Isn't a clean break the best thing?'

There's no such thing as a clean break. Haven't you discovered that in the lonely days and aching nights?

'Do you have anything else lined up?' Mr. Pendry asked.

'No, I guess I don't,' she said, picking up the pen. 'So what happens now?'

'You just keep on running the shop. I dare say they'll send someone to see you sooner or later.'

She lay awake all night, knowing that she'd signed because she was a coward. She couldn't face another break so soon after the last one. She would see out her contract and separate herself from her beloved shop inch by inch.

Yet again, as she'd done so many times since returning to London, she asked herself why she'd taken such a stubborn stand against the man she couldn't stop loving? Truth to tell, she'd always considered herself a touch on the wimpish side. So how had she found the weapons in her hands?

Because Marco had shown them to her.

He'd told her that she was strong and brave and independent, and it was true. The neglect and loneliness that had marked her life had taught her how to be alone, but she hadn't known it until Marco revealed her strengths to her. He'd proved that she could do without the father she'd yearned for, and the next step was the knowledge that she could do without anyone.

Now she could do without Marco, because he'd taught her how.

Next day she overslept. It was Mrs Gilchrist's day off so she couldn't have picked a worse moment to be late. As she hastened to the shop, she crossed her fingers and prayed to whichever deity protected disorganised antique dealers not to let A&J send their representative today.

She knew her prayers weren't being answered when she arrived to find the front door standing open. She'd been beaten to it. She was late. Just like that other time. She could just imagine what Marco would say to this.

And that was exactly what he said as he emerged from her cubicle at the back of the shop to stand regarding her sardonically.

'Dammit Harriet, not again! Are you never on time?'

CHAPTER TWELVE

'I DON'T believe this,' Harriet said, setting down her things to confront him. 'What are you doing here?'

'Haven't you worked it out yet?'

'Allum & Jonsey—?'

'A tiny firm who were glad to let me take them over.'

'And if they hadn't been glad, you'd have taken over anyway.'

'No, I'd have found another firm. I needed a front. You wouldn't have sold if you'd known it was me.'

'In other words, this is another of your exercises in control. Sorry Marco, it's not going to work. I'm through.'

He held up the contract she'd signed only the previous day, committing her to run the shop for six months. 'What about this?'

'Sue me!'

'I will if you make me, but you won't. You're a woman of your word. This place needs you.

Nobody else can run it. Between us we'll make it as profitable as it ought to be.'

Harriet gave an incredulous laugh. 'You want *me?* A woman who can't tell a fake from an original? Surely not.'

She had the satisfaction of seeing him redden. 'What do you want me to say? That I was wrong about that? All right, I'll say it. That necklace was a fake. My father sold the original years ago. My mother says you're the only person ever to notice.'

Harriet's face lightened. 'How is she?'

'I have strict instructions to send her news of you. I'll do that later. For the moment we have to do some serious talking.'

'Well, I won't try to defend my accounts to you—'

'No, they're beyond defence.'

'Because you already knew the worst in advance. You're crazy, you know that?'

His eyes gleamed. 'I never do anything without a good reason.'

'You can't have a good reason for being here.'

'That's for me to say,' he said briskly. 'We had a deal. The loan was to be repaid in easy stages, instead you choose to deprive yourself of everything you love, to do it in one go. That gives me a certain responsibility.'

'You haven't—'

'Will you just be quiet while I'm speaking? When I want to hear what you have to say, I'll ask. I have a responsibility to you and I'm going to deal with it. I'll teach you to be a shrewd businesswoman if it turns us both grey-haired. In time you'll make enough to buy this place back from me, and then I won't have to reproach myself with having harmed you.'

'Can I speak now?' she snapped.

'If it's important.'

'All that is very conscientious of you—'

'Conscientiousness is the corner of good business. Now, I suggest you make some tea and we'll discuss your stock buying. Some of the web sites you visit look interesting.'

'You accessed my account? How?'

'I hacked in, of course.'

'Of course,' she murmured.

'If you'd been here on time, it would have been easier,' he said crisply, and something in his tone made her realise that this man was now her employer.

From then on she had no chance to forget it. Marco settled in as though he'd come for a long stay, taking a room at the Ritz Hotel, hiring a car, arriving at the shop early, leaving late. If Harriet suspected that he had come for her he made it hard for her to believe it. He gave her a crash course in financial management, with no concessions to whatever might have been between them. When he'd finished tearing her business practices to shreds he demolished the reputation of her accountant.

'He's been so much in awe of your academic knowledge that he's let you get away with accounting murder.'

'He's a dear old boy—'

'So I would have guessed. You don't need a dear old boy, you need someone who can keep you on a tight rein. What's this?' He was pointing at some squiggles in one of the ledgers.

'That's my code.'

'Translate,' he snapped.

Seething, she did so.

'Fine,' he said. 'That's lucid enough, but I'm not clairvoyant. How do I know what it means unless you explain?'

'I always write up the details later.'

'Do it now.'

'Why do you have to be a slave-driver over every detail?'

'Because, while you may be all kinds of an antiquarian genius, when it comes to the simplest commercial transaction *you are a bird-brained idiot*.'

'*I know that!*'

Silence. He was breathing hard.

'Fine!' he snapped. 'Then at last we're agreed on something. It makes a good starting point.'

'Why do we have to agree on anything? We never did before. Why don't you just install the new accountant to keep an eye on me when you've gone home?'

'I'm not going home until I've taught you how not to bankrupt yourself.'

'You mean, bankrupt you?'

For once he was shaken. 'Yes—yes, that's what I meant.'

'But you can't stay here. You should be in Rome this minute, fighting for that partnership.'

He shrugged. 'I clinched that before I left.'

'So you've got it?'

'Yes, I've got it.' He was writing something.

'The youngest partner, just as you wanted. Congratulations!'

'Thank you!' he said shortly.

Of course he'd got exactly what he wanted. Everything neat and orderly. He'd sorted out his career, now he would deal with the little matter of his conscience, then he would go home and put her behind him.

But that was what she wanted him to do.

So she had no complaints. If there was one thing she was sure of, it was that.

* * *

'How do you buy stock?' he asked her one day. 'You can't always use the internet.'

'I use it rarely. Travelling the country is better.'

'When do we go?'

Next day they set off for a country house south of London. The owner had fallen on hard times, had sold the house to the local council, and was raising what he could from the contents.

'He won't get much for these, I'm afraid,' Harriet said regretfully as she examined the rather dull collection of items. 'And he's such a sweet little man.' She looked sympathetically across at the owner, a plump, white-haired man with a sad face.

'Anything of interest to us?' Marco asked.

'Well, this vase looks—' she stopped, examining an ornate glass vase. Marco saw her flicker of interest, quickly suppressed, like the professional she was.

'What?' he said.

'Genuine Venetian twelfth century,' she said quietly. 'Worth about fifty grand.'

'But the reserve price is only two grand.'

'I know. The owner can't have any idea what it's worth.'

'So you've spotted a real bargain. I'm impressed.'

The auctioneer banged his gavel. 'Take your places please, ladies and gentlemen.'

Marco bagged two seats in the front and looked around for Harriet. After a moment he saw her talking earnestly to the owner while the auctioneer stood listening, wide-eyed.

I don't believe this, he thought. *I simply don't believe it, not even of her.*

The auctioneer banged his gavel again.

'Ladies and gentlemen, I have to announce that Lot 43 now has a reserve price of fifty thousand…'

From the groan that went up behind him Marco judged that other dealers had spotted the same thing, and had kept quiet.

But they weren't Harriet, Marco thought with a private smile.

She was hailing him from the door, indicating that they should leave.

'We're not interested in anything else here,' she said as he joined her outside.

'Aren't *we?*'

'No, *we're* not.'

'I gather you told him?'

'I had to. That dear little old man, he was almost crying. He said it'll make all the difference to his retirement. Hey, what are you doing?' she protested as he grabbed her arm and began to hustle her.

'Getting you to safety before one of the other dealers murders you.'

'Or doing it yourself?'

He didn't answer this, except with a look.

When they were out in the sun she faced him, half-sheepish, half-defiant.

'I couldn't do anything else, don't you see? He's such an innocent, I couldn't just take the money when he needs it so much—'

'But Harriet, dear crazy Harriet, that's not how you do business.'

'It's how *I* do business. So you'd better fire me.'

'No, I'm glad you told him,' he said with a strange smile. 'If you'd done anything else, you wouldn't have been Harriet.'

It was early evening as they drove back to London.

'Now we need something to eat,' Marco said. 'I suppose I can't suggest that you invite me to your home for beans on toast. Since I'm your employer that might be ''sexual harassment''.'

'I'll risk it. After one taste of my cooking you won't be up to anything.'

'Witty lady!' he said admiringly. 'Come on, give me directions.'

Her home was a tiny one-bedroomed apartment an hour away, in a cheaper part of town.

Harriet wondered how it appeared to Marco who'd grown up in the luxury of the Villa Calvani. She saw him looking about the cramped rooms, but he said nothing.

She spared him beans on toast and made spaghetti, letting him create the sauce. Conversation was spasmodic and about nothing in particular. It had been a good day, and now neither of them knew how to end it.

He'd been very unfair to her, she thought. She'd meant to be strong, but that was when she'd thought he would be far away. How was she supposed to be strong when she was seeing him day after day, close to him, hearing his voice? And when she looked up to find him watching her, only to see him turn away without words, leaving the memory of the look in his eyes and a torturing feeling of delight—there had to be a way to defend herself against that, if only she could find it.

It wasn't fair that her love for him should flower more strongly than ever before. But love wasn't fair. If he went away now and left her to struggle with her misery that wouldn't be fair either. But it could happen.

She was on edge, wondering what he would do and how she would react. Why was he really here?

In the end he did something totally unexpected. As she was putting dishes into the sink he came up behind her and laid his hands on her shoulders. She waited, half hoping, half-unsure. After staying like that a moment, not moving, he slid one arm across her chest, drawing her back against him, and dropping his head to lay it gently against the side of her neck. She could feel his lips, lightly touching her skin, but he didn't kiss her. It was neither a passionate nor even a very romantic movement. He simply looked weary and disheartened, and she suddenly remembered when she'd found him sleeping rough in the garden, and he'd put his arms around her and rested his head, as though in her he found a refuge.

Slowly she put up her hand to touch his and they stayed like that for a long moment. Then he released her and went away. When she went to find him he was kneeling before her bookcase, reading the titles.

After that she made them both coffee, he exclaimed about the time, and went home.

Marco didn't come into the shop every day, and she supposed he was using the time to keep up with his work in Rome. One morning when she was alone she went into her cubby-hole to make some tea. Above the clatter of china she didn't hear the shop door open and someone come in, and emerged to find a young woman standing there. She was expensively dressed, about thirty, dark-haired, dark-eyed, pretty in a lush way, and about six months pregnant. She had the smile of someone who was deeply content with her life.

'You are *la Signorina d'Estino*?' She had a strong Italian accent and spoke carefully, like someone feeling her way in the language.

'Yes, I'm Harriet d'Estino. Can I show you something?'

'Oh, no, I do not come to buy, but to talk. About Marco.'

'I don't understand.'

'My name is Alessandra,' the young woman said simply. 'And I come to tell you how important it is that you marry him.'

Harriet stared, and the only words that came into her head were, 'Let's have a cup of tea.'

When they were seated Harriet said, 'Would you mind repeating that?'

'I say you must marry Marco. You think I'm *pazza*, no?'

'No, I don't think you're crazy, but I do wonder why Marco's marriage matters to you.'

'Why should I worry about a man in my past? And yet I do. Perhaps I feel a little guilty. Since we parted life has gone well for me, not for him. My friends who know him say that it was as if he shrivelled up inside, and began to keep the world at a distance. For that, I am, perhaps, to blame.'

'It's not your fault if you changed your mind,' Harriet ventured.

'No, but I should have had the courage to break our engagement honestly. You see, Marco feels too much. He *minds* too much, everything is too important. He acts otherwise. To the world he is a man who feels nothing, but the world doesn't know him.' She looked shrewdly at Harriet. 'But I think you know.'

'Yes,' Harriet said. 'Quite soon after I went to Italy I began to sense what he was hiding. He even hides it from himself.'

'Ah, that's bad. That too is my fault. Once he hid nothing. He overwhelmed me, and gradually I began to feel that it was more than I wanted. He was jealous, my whole life must belong to him. I became bored, and my love died. I fell in love with another man, but I didn't tell Marco. I worried about what he would do and besides, the man was married. His wife had money, he didn't want to leave her—'

Alessandra shrugged. Harriet maintained a diplomatic silence. She was on the verge of learning the key to Marco and she wasn't going to risk losing her chance through showing her opinion of this self-centred woman.

'Then I discovered that I was pregnant,' Alessandra continued. 'Marco saw me have a dizzy spell, and guessed. He assumed the baby was his—'

'Could it have been?'

'You mean was I sleeping with them both? Yes. The timing made Harvey more likely, but Marco didn't know about him so he just took it for granted that the child was his, and immediately began to plan our wedding. I argued for a delay but—you know how he can be.'

Harriet nodded.

'He was overjoyed—I tried to tell him the truth—but I confess I was scared of him. He can be a very frightening man. There is much love in him, and much hate when his anger is roused. He feels everything too much. That's why he struggles to hide it. If people knew they would think him weak and use it against him.'

'So what happened?' Harriet asked.

'One day Marco returned early from a business trip and came to my apartment without warning. He let himself in with his own key. Harvey was with me. We were making love.'

Harriet winced and closed her eyes.

'Of course it came out, about the child,' Alessandra said.

'What did he say?'

'Nothing. Not a word. He just stood there

looking a man who was dying. Then he walked out. That was the last time I saw him. He sent me a note saying that he'd told people the wedding was off by mutual consent. Both of us had realised that we'd made a mistake. Of course I agreed to that.

'By that time Harvey's wife had found out about us and her brothers were on the warpath. He's English, so we ran away to England, and our son was born here. He really is Harvey's child. We did a test to make sure. But nobody in Rome knew the exact date of his birth, so they couldn't count back and realise that I must have betrayed Marco during our engagement. In Rome they still believe it was ''mutual consent'' and I'm glad for Marco's sake. It would have killed him if the truth was known. People would have laughed.

'There were rumours, you see. People had warned him that I had a roving eye, and he'd refused to listen. He is a loyal and faithful man, and that is how he loves.'

'Not any more. I think all that died, and now he doesn't know how to love.'

'No,' Alessandra said urgently. 'No man with his capacity for love really loses it. He hides it, he tries to deny it, but it's always there. One day he was bound to fall in love again. I'm glad it was with you. I think you'll be good for him.'

'You're wrong. Marco isn't in love with me.'

'Nonsense, of course he is. What do you think he's been doing here for weeks when he should have been in Rome fighting for that partnership?'

'But he got the partnership before he left—' Harriet protested. Alessandra's raised eyebrows gave her a strange feeling. *'Didn't he?'*

'Not according to my cousin who works there. It's gone to somebody else. It's already been announced.'

Harriet had been pacing but now she sat down abruptly. 'Why did you come here?' she asked.

'To clear my conscience and try to put right the harm I did him. I owe him that. Don't give up on him Harriet. He couldn't endure it a second time.'

Two days passed with no sign of him. In that time she ran the whole gamut of emotions from joy, hope, disbelief, despair. After what Alessandra had told her she urgently needed to see Marco, to look into his eyes and discover if it was true that he loved her.

At last she heard a foot on the step that was unmistakably his, and looked up smiling, but the smile faded. This was Marco at his most formal, dressed for departure in an overcoat. He looked as though he hadn't slept.

'Are you taking a trip?' she asked.

'I'm going back to Rome.'

'For a few days?'

'For good. I shan't be coming back.'

The thud over her heart was like a punch. 'I see.'

'But before I leave I must give you this.' He took an envelope from his briefcase and handed it to her.

Moving mechanically she pulled out a paper and tried to read it, but the words danced before her eyes. Only one thought possessed her. He was going away, and in a few moments her life would be over. Somehow there must be a way to prevent him but her brain had become a terrible blank. The thudding of her heart seemed to fill the world.

'Read it,' he said quietly.

She tried to concentrate on the paper, and this time she made out figures, the amount of her debt to him. It was a receipt.

'This paper says I own the shop—but how can I?'

There was a look of intolerable sadness in his eyes. 'I could say that you repaid me what you owed, if it didn't offend me to speak of your gifts to me in terms of money. You've given me so much more than you'll ever know, so much more than I deserve.'

He looked around him. 'When I think how I came here that first day, so sure of myself, so confident that everything could be arranged to suit me, I want to shudder at the man I was then. He's gone now, thanks to you. This is so little in return.' He indicated the paper. 'I'd hoped to give it to you—well—under happier circumstances. Now I think that's not going to happen. I want you to have it anyway.'

'But—' she stammered, frantically trying to find the words '—you can't just leave the shop with me. I'll make a mess of it again.'

'Not after all I've taught you,' he said with a faint smile. He brushed a stray wisp of hair back from her forehead.

'I wasn't a very good pupil.'

'You were the best kind of pupil. One who taught her teacher far more than he taught her. I shall carry your lessons all my life.'

'I shan't carry yours,' she said wildly. 'I'll forget them and go bankrupt. Besides, what became of the sharp-eyed businessman? You can't just give me all this money. Think of the shocking tax.'

'Tax?' he echoed, trying to keep up with her.

'Never forget the tax angle. You taught me that.'

He didn't answer for a moment. He'd understood now that she was following some new track of her own, and he was trying to keep up.

'What—are you saying?' he asked quietly at last.

'You talked about "happier circumstances". I don't know why you're so sure they're not going to happen. Maybe you've jumped to conclusions about that. But I think—as a wedding present, it would be treated much more favourably.'

He looked at her for a long moment before saying slowly, 'But the lady I love won't marry me. She told me so, and I've come to see that she might be right. I have no right to even try to persuade her.'

Harriet could hardly breathe. 'She might change her mind—just to secure a tax break.'

Slowly he shook his head. 'That's no good. It's not the right reason.'

'I was only joking.'

'I know, but there are some things you shouldn't joke about. They matter too much.'

'Business?'

'Love. I love you Harriet, and if you can't say the same just let me go quickly—'

'I can say it a million times over,' she said, touching his cheek. He immediately seized her hand and turned his head to kiss it. There was a desperate eagerness in his eyes.

'Tell me that you love me,' he pleaded. 'I need to hear you say it.'

She raised her other hand so that his face was held between them. 'I love you with all my heart and soul. I always will.'

She was in his arms before the words were quite out, having the breath kissed out of her in an embrace as crushing as he'd ever given her.

'I thought I'd lost you,' he said huskily. 'All the time you were in Rome I knew I was losing you and I didn't know how to stop it happening. I loved you but I couldn't tell you. I had the words ready a thousand times but lost my nerve. I didn't have the courage. I'm a coward, that's the truth and you may as well know it.'

'Marco, darling, please—'

'No, don't stop me. I want the truth there between us. Once before I—'

'I know.' She touched his lips gently. 'Alessandra. She came to see me.'

'She was here? In this shop? When?'

'A few days ago. She told me about the partnership you lost. You said you had it in the bag.'

'I had to. If I'd told you I was giving up the chance to be with you it would have been like blackmailing you.'

'But the partnership—it means everything to you—'

'No, you mean everything to me. There'll be other partnerships, but I knew this was my last chance with you. If I failed to win your love there'd never be another chance, and I couldn't face that.' He hesitated before saying awkwardly, 'What else did Alessandra tell you?'

'Everything. Do you mind?'

He shook his head. 'Now you know. I'm glad. I was a coward there too. I wasn't going to give anyone the chance to get to me again. I told myself that was a kind of strength, not seeing it for the weakness it really was.

'But you made everything different. I was so happy whenever I was with you. I tried to rationalise the happiness away, but it possessed me. I wanted to tell you but I couldn't. Then I tried to let you know without words, but I never seemed to get it right. And that night we were together, was so wonderful—so wonderful—I knew I was lost, as I'd sworn never to be again.

'I was so arrogant it shames me. I knew I couldn't let you go, but I thought I could have you on my own terms, without a surrender. And that evening in Venice, when we were walking, every word you said seemed designed to warn me off. You were planning to go away, so I tried to back you into a corner, force you to marry me, and I lost you completely.

'I didn't know how to get you back. This was the best I could think of, but you were so wary of me, I thought I had no hope. I was going to leave and set you free of me. That was the only way left to prove a love I thought you didn't want.'

'I'll always want your love. Never leave me, my darling.'

'You don't know what you're doing,' he said as he rained kisses over her face. 'You'll regret it—'

'Never!'

'I can't do things by half,' he murmured. 'I'll always be possessive. I'll want all of you—'

'All,' she whispered joyfully.

'You'll have to fight me—promise me that you will. Otherwise you might start to hate me and I couldn't endure that.'

'I'll fight you,' she promised.

'And I shall learn from you,' he said seriously. 'You've taught me so much. Go on teaching me. Be my mentor, keep me safe.' He dropped his head so that his mouth lay against her palm.

'Safe in my heart,' she whispered. 'Safe in my heart my beloved—for always.'

...there's more to the story!

Superromance.
A *big* satisfying read about unforgettable characters. Each month we offer *six* very different stories that range from family drama to adventure and mystery, from highly emotional stories to romantic comedies—and much more! Stories about people you'll believe in and care about. Stories too compelling to put down....

Our authors are among today's *best* romance writers. You'll find familiar names and talented newcomers. Many of them are award winners—and you'll see why!

If you want the biggest and best in romance fiction, you'll get it from Superromance!

Emotional, Exciting, Unexpected...

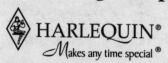

HARLEQUIN®
*M*akes any time special ®

Harlequin®
Historical

From rugged lawmen and valiant knights to defiant heiresses and spirited frontierswomen, Harlequin Historicals will capture your imagination with their dramatic scope, passion and adventure.

Harlequin Historicals . . . they're too good to miss!

HHDIR1